"Let's get you out of here!"

Bolan and Lily ran from the smokehouse. The men in the guard tower were pointing and screaming, but no one on the ground was paying them any attention.

The Executioner spoke into his phone. "Fatso, hit the tower, then fire at the house."

"I have bad guys coming my way!" Nyin responded, but the grenade launcher down in Ta village thumped. The two men in the tower noticed Bolan and Lily as they reached the palisade. One began screaming, while the other raised a rifle.

The grenade launcher thumped again as Lily wriggled through the hole. Bolan grabbed her hand and ran for the tree line. Behind them gray gas and white smoke were blanketing U Than's fortress in a fog of war. It was a war that had just begun, and tomorrow it would become a hunt. U Than was going to want payback.

It was over five hundred miles to the border of Thailand.

MACK BOLAN ®

The Executioner

The Don Pendleton's Executioner®

MISSION TO BURMA

A GOLD EAGLE BOOK FROM

WORLDWIDE®

TORONTO • NEW YORK • LONDON
AMSTERDAM • PARIS • SYDNEY • HAMBURG
STOCKHOLM • ATHENS • TOKYO • MILAN
MADRID • WARSAW • BUDAPEST • AUCKLAND

First edition November 2008

ISBN-13: 978-0-373-64360-8
ISBN-10:   0-373-64360-8

Special thanks and acknowledgment to
Charles Rogers for his contribution to this work.

MISSION TO BURMA

Printed in U.S.A.

Nothing gives one person so much advantage over another as to remain always cool and unruffled under all circumstances.

—Thomas Jefferson,
1743–1826

No matter how dangerous or deadly my foe, I will not waver in my pursuit.

—Mack Bolan

THE
MACK BOLAN

LEGEND

Nothing less than a war could have fashioned the destiny of the man called Mack Bolan. Bolan earned the Executioner title in the jungle hell of Vietnam.

But this soldier also wore another name—Sergeant Mercy. He was so tagged because of the compassion he showed to wounded comrades-in-arms and Vietnamese civilians.

Mack Bolan's second tour of duty ended prematurely when he was given emergency leave to return home and bury his family, victims of the Mob. Then he declared a one-man war against the Mafia.

He confronted the Families head-on from coast to coast, and soon a hope of victory began to appear. But Bolan had broken society's every rule. That same society started gunning for this elusive warrior—to no avail.

So Bolan was offered amnesty to work within the system against terrorism. This time, as an employee of Uncle Sam, Bolan became Colonel John Phoenix. With a command center at Stony Man Farm in Virginia, he and his new allies—Able Team and Phoenix Force—waged relentless war on a new adversary: the KGB.

But when his one true love, April Rose, died at the hands of the Soviet terror machine, Bolan severed all ties with Establishment authority.

Now, after a lengthy lone-wolf struggle and much soul-searching, the Executioner has agreed to enter an "arm's-length" alliance with his government once more, reserving the right to pursue personal missions in his Everlasting War.

1

Flight 402, Burmese airspace

Lily Na knew she was in trouble. All intelligence agencies kept a few beautiful women on the payroll, and Lily was the most beautiful spy Taiwanese intelligence had embedded in the People's Republic of China. But jade-green eyes, breast augmentation and the 108 acknowledged Taoist methods of seduction would not save her from the heat-seeking missiles of the PRC jet fighters flanking her flight.

Her bodyguard returned from the consulting the pilot. Jun-Sui was nicknamed "Ox Boy" for the breadth of his shoulders and his massive strength. He was a master of white-ape kung fu and a deadly shot with the silenced machine pistol in his shoulder holster. He bowed to Lily with profound respect. "The pilot believes the jet fighters are about to fire upon us. He and I both agree you should bail out now while the opportunity still presents itself."

The short flight from Kunming Airport in China to Calcutta should have been a breeze. Then the laptop containing the PRC ballistic missile reentry vehicle guidance technology would be turned over to the CIA station office, after which Lily had planned a well-deserved yoga retreat in Costa Rica. The arrival of a pair of Chinese SU-30MKK fighters had ended her dreams of hot yoga, hot tubs and the pink sand beaches of the Nicoyan Peninsula. The former Union of Burma had nothing in its air force capable of dealing with the massive Chinese fighters invading Burmese airspace, nor would they risk their beleaguered economy by protesting to their biggest trading partner.

The People's Republic wanted this flight, and they were going to have it. They wanted it turned around and landing across the border at Baoshon Airbase. They would settle for a smoking crater in the Kumon Highlands.

Lily inclined her head slightly at Ox Boy. "I will bail out."

Ox Boy bowed again. Lily slipped her laptop into a padded pouch and followed him back to the galley. Terrified passengers followed their progress but stayed strapped into their seats as the pilot had directed. Ox Boy yanked open the hatch that dropped into the luggage compartment below. They climbed down, and he pulled a parachute rig out of a locker and helped Lily shrug into it. "Wait until the last possible moment to open your parachute."

Lily slapped the buckles of her rig and tightened the straps. "When would that be?"

Ox Boy clicked open his cell phone and had a short, cryptic conversation with the pilot and then clicked it shut. "Count to twenty."

"Very well."

Ox Boy shoved night-vision goggles down over her eyes as Lily checked the loads in her Browning Hi-Power pistol.

"Turn on your transponder."

Lily pulled her crucifix out from under the high collar of her dress. She gave it a hard squeeze at the apex of its arms and then tucked it back in. Once the tiny transmitter was activated, certain surveillance satellites of the United States, the United Kingdom and Taiwan would be combing Southeast Asia for its tiny but distinctive signature. The lurid red lights turned off, and the baggage compartment whirled into a hurricane as the loading door opened.

The pilot's voice spoke over the intercom in Mandarin. "Agent Na, we have been given our last warning. We are about to be fired upon."

"Very well, I will—"

Ox Boy slammed both hands against Lily's back and shoved her out the door.

She gasped in shock, but training took over. She arched her body hard and thrust out bent arms and legs as the jet wash flung her about like laundry. Flight 402 shot away westward with a roar as she stabilized her free fall. She jerked involuntarily as the two SU-30MMK fighters screamed past, but a tumbling human body was virtually no target to a fighter's air combat radar. Lily plunged through space as the jets flew on toward India at six hundred miles per hour.

The clouds flashed as if they were lit up by lightning as both fighters cut loose with their 30 mm cannons. The cloud cover in the west went from orange to white and then to red as Flight 402 broke apart and exploded beneath the automatic cannon onslaught. Lily winced against the sonic booms as the fighter jets turned and went supersonic to return to base. She had lost her drop count, but the Kumon Mountains were rushing up beneath her with disturbing speed. Lily brought her feet together, kicked off her high heels and faced facts.

Regal, voluptuous and green-eyed as she was, her problem was that from the get-go she had been designed to be insertable, deniable and expendable. Any extraction assets in the civil-war-ridden mountain and river valleys of Burma would have to be the same. The upper tier of the jungle canopy of the Kumon Mountains rushed toward Lily's silk-stockinged feet and she wondered what, if any, kind of man might be sent to save her.

2

Mack Bolan stared at the 8 x 10 glossy of Lily Na. She was Taiwanese National Security Bureau and undoubtedly straight out of "Mystical 110," or 110 Yangteh Boulevard on Yang Ming Mountain outside Taipei. It was the address of NSB headquarters, a place where no visitors were allowed, and people who did visit usually came in late at night and often never left. Miss Na was undoubtedly one of the NSB's secret weapons, probably from the Chinese Mainland Maneuvers Committee.

Bolan looked up at Hal Brognola. "Rescue missions aren't normally my kind of thing, Hal."

"Yeah, but what about the woman?" Brognola countered. "I know for a fact she's your kind of thing."

Bolan returned his gaze to Na's picture. She was undeniably erotic. "Still not my kind of mission."

"Yeah, I know." The big Fed gnawed on his unlit cigar. "But the stakes are high on this one."

Bolan knew the stakes were about as high as they got in the world of international espionage. The United States and Taiwan very badly wanted the ballistic-missile-defense information. It was information the Chinese government wanted back even more, so much that they'd downed an entire jet full of innocent people over Burmese airspace. They were working on the forty-eighth hour of her disappearance, but her personal transponder was still signaling.

"You know the government has people and agencies who train for exactly this kind of spook-extraction bullshit," Bolan argued.

"Yeah, I know." Brognola sighed. "They've already tried and failed."

Bolan raised an eyebrow. "Really."

"Yeah, actually the CIA was Johnny-on-the-spot on this one. Within twenty-four hours, they sent in two paramilitary rescue teams. One was compromised and stopped at the border before ever setting a boot in country. The second was smaller, a couple of advisers who parachuted in and met up with mobilized local assets. It's been twelve hours since we've heard from them. We have to assume they've been captured or killed."

Two teams in twenty-four hours was not good. "I think you have to assume they were compromised."

"That's right. That's why the President wants to send in someone who's outside of normal channels."

Bolan had to admit he was about as far from normal channels as one could get, short of hiring extraterrestrials. "You know, I don't speak Burmese, Hal. I don't think I even know any of the swear words."

"It's a former British colony," Brognola said. "Everyone there speaks a little English."

"That was sixty years ago." Bolan considered what he knew about the Union of Myanmar, known by most Westerners as Burma. The government was an utterly corrupt military junta that ruled with an iron fist. Human rights were nearly nonexistent. Human trafficking was some of the worst in Asia. Like most of Southeast Asia, the country was a patchwork of mountains and river valleys with dozens of oppressed ethnic minorities. Some of the minorities were large enough and well enough armed that the rule of the government only extended as far as their artillery could reach outside the big cities. Burma was also ground zero of Asia's Golden Triangle of opium production. The warlords ruled their areas like medieval fiefs, alternately fighting with and doing business with government and rebel alike. "You do realize I'm over six feet tall, white and have blue eyes?"

"Actually I've noticed that about you," Brognola admitted.

"So I can't exactly blend in. If the first villager who sees me doesn't turn me into the government as a spy, then they're going to sell me to the drug lords as a DEA agent."

"The President and I were both hoping you might do that lurking-in-the-dark thing you do so well." Brognola brightened. "Besides, we have a local asset to assist you."

"Hal, the Chinese found out Miss Na and the data were on the plane and shot it down. You had one CIA paramilitary team stopped at the border, and a CIA lead team of local auxiliaries has disappeared. There's a leak someplace, and you're going to have to forgive me if I'm not trusting local CIA or Taiwanese assets."

"I wouldn't trust them, either." Brognola smiled. "So he's neither."

"Care to explain that?"

"Sure, like you said, there's a leak somewhere. I'd like to think it's Taiwan, but we can't be sure. The President wants you because you're outside normal channels. That made sense to me, so I went outside normal channels to get you some local backup."

"Where'd you go?"

"I called David McCarter."

McCarter was the team leader of Stony Man Farm's elite international strike force. He was also a former member of the British SAS.

Bolan smiled. "He contacted British intelligence."

"Well, like I said, they used to own the place, so I figured they must have a few people keeping their hands in. MI-6 was kind enough to get in contact with this guy." Hal handed over a file. In it was the picture of a bald, buck-toothed little man with a belly like Buddha jammed into a Hawaiian shirt and khaki shorts. He was grinning into the camera. "His name is Fat Sho Nyin. His call sign with British intelligence is 'Fatso.' Don't let his looks fool you. He was a sergeant in the Burmese Airborne Unit."

"So what's his story?"

"He was operating in the northern mountains, in the Sagaing Division about a decade ago. He fell in love with a Naga tribeswoman. The local opium lord came in and wiped out her village. She and Nyin's illegitimate child were killed. Nyin's commander had a business arrangement with the drug lord and did nothing. The Naga are headhunters. The practice was banned in 1991, but rumor is some of the good old boys up in the hills still stick to the old ways. Rumor is Nyin got together a few of his woman's relatives, got tattooed and inducted into the tribe, and they went and got a little payback. Most U.S. heroin comes from Afghanistan and Mexico, but a lot of the heroin in England is still coming in from the Golden Triangle. Nyin's been one of the guys on the ground for MI-6's antinarcotic Southeast Asia sector for a decade. Mostly, he works against the drug trade, but apparently he's given them military intelligence from time to time, as well as helping break up a few slavery rings. He'd be your liaison among the locals." Brognola cleared his throat. "If you go…"

"Anything else you need to tell me?"

"Well, now that you mention it, NSA has picked up some chatter."

"What kind of chatter?"

"They believe the Indian government is aware of the situation and possibly even taking action."

Bolan considered that. "India is a strategic ally of ours. Particularly against China. You'd think we'd be allies on this one."

"So you'd think. But knowledge of China's latest generation strategic nuclear missiles is vital to India. They lost a border war with them in the 1960s and still have 'incidents' with China every year. India might not wait for us to secure the information and share it. They'll want to get hold of it first, and then probably trade the U.S. and Taiwan something for it economically. Chatter is India may have already deployed assets, and you shouldn't necessarily expect them to be helpful or even friendly."

Bolan sat back in his chair. "Great."

"Listen, Mack, you don't have to—"

"I'll have to HALO in."

Brognola blinked. "You'll do it?"

"Yeah." Bolan nodded. "I'll do it."

Kumon Mountains

BOLAN LOPED through the trees. It had taken eighteen hours for him to get geared up and to the Diego Garcia Airbase in the Indian Ocean. It took the B-2 Stealth "Spirit" bomber another six to get over northern Burma. Burmese air defense had no radars that could detect the bat-winged bomber, and even if they lucked out it was unlikely they could scramble anything in time to catch it. The problem with a Stealth bomber was it was not designed as a passenger plane. Bolan had ridden in a pressurized, coffin-size pod that had been adapted to fit into one of the rotary launcher assemblies the bombers used to launch cruise missiles. The pod had been just big enough to hold Bolan and his equipment. The belly of the Spirit of Texas had opened, and the transport pod had ejected and fallen free at thirty thousand feet. Bolan had opened the pod at twenty-seven thousand and deployed his chute. He had flown thirty miles into the Kumon Mountains and landed in the designated clearing on his map.

Fatso was nowhere to be found.

Bolan looked at his wrist. Strapped to it was a PDA with a phone feature, but basically Bolan almost had a supercomputer on his wrist. He was using the GPS to navigate his way toward the transponder. He tapped an icon and spoke into his satellite link. "Base, this is Striker. What have we got on infrared imaging?"

Barbara Price came back instantly. The Farm's mission controller was watching Bolan's progress on no less than three U.S. satellites. The Chinese data was that big. "Striker, this is Base. I have a possible heat source a hundred yards due east of your position."

"Copy that. Give me feed."

"Copy that, Striker."

A red blob appeared on Bolan's screen marking his target. A green blob represented him, along with a superimposed grid giving him distance.

Bolan slung his rifle. There had been no point to trying to blend in as Burmese, so Bolan had cherry picked his equipment. He carried a highly modified Steyr Scout Rifle. A suppressor tube covered most of the already short, fluted barrel, and it was loaded with subsonic ammunition. The bolt-action rifle had a 10-round magazine. Its optical sight was set forward of the action to give long-eye relief, allowing the operator to keep both eyes open and take in the full field of view, as well as look through the sight while using night-vision gear. The action was glass-on-oil smooth and the trigger tuned to a glass-rod break. It was a sharp-shooter's weapon rather than a sniper's rifle, the weapon of a skirmisher rather than an assassin. Bolan's rifle also happened to have an M-203 grenade launcher mounted beneath the fore-stock for serious social occasions such as needing to break contact, and he carried a bandolier of grenades slung across one shoulder. His Beretta 93-R machine pistol was strapped to his thigh, but that was not the weapon he went for.

Bolan drew his tomahawk in one hand and his Cold Steel Out-doorsman knife in the other as he ran wide around his adversary. Bolan was going to have to lurk rather than infiltrate and considered both implements much more as tools than weapons. However, a bullet was never sure, and a man could still flail with his throat cut.

There was no surer way of silencing a sentry than sinking a tomahawk into the back of his head.

Bolan squelched his electronic devices and moved in for the kill. Most people thought of Southeast Asia as one vast, green mass of impenetrable vegetation, but much of it, Burma in particular, was much more rolling low mountains of hardwood forest.

Bolan could see his prey in his night-vision goggles. A man was crouched on a little promontory holding a rifle. Bolan noted the short, curved blade of a *dha* sword thrust through his belt. The man knelt in a stand of trees that made a sheltering cathedral on the little knoll and looked down on the valley below. It was a perfect hunter's point. Bolan's boots made no noise in the soft soil as he approached. The man jerked in alarm as the Executioner whipped the bottom edge of his tomahawk under his chin and yanked him backward. The man froze as the point of Bolan's blade pressed against his liver. "Nyin?"

"Shit, Hot rod! Don't sneak up on a brother like that!"

Bolan withdrew his steel, and the man sagged and turned. Fat Sho Nyin wiped his sweating bald head and exposed his buck teeth in a shaky smile of relief. He took in the goggle-eyed, weapon-laden and camouflaged warrior looming over him and shook his head. "God damn! Uncle Sam ain't playing around!"

"No, he's not," Bolan agreed. He sheathed his weapons and held out his hand. "MI-6 has a lot of good things to say about you. My name is Cooper."

Fatso clapped his palm happily into Bolan's hand. "Bullshit GI! But you go ahead and call me Fatso. I will call you Cooper."

Bolan shrugged. "Make it Coop."

"Coop." Nyin savored the familiar diminutive. "Sorry I was not at extraction sight. Some assholes came by."

"What kind of assholes?"

Nyin's smile dimmed in wattage. "U Than assholes."

Bolan knew all about U Than. He was an opium warlord, and they were deep in his territory, which was where Lily's transponder signal was transmitting from. The good news was that U Than was in league with the heroin syndicates in Thailand rather than the triads in China. Of course, ten or twenty million Chinese yuan notes could change that allegiance, but at least he wasn't going to immediately go goose-stepping to Beijing and hand over Lily without some profitable negotiation first. U Than's problem was that while he ruled his area, he was surrounded by three ethnic groups that considered him their traditional enemy. He had a private army of his own and some backing by some high-ranking army officers, but his neighbors and even his serfs were highly warlike and given to rebellion at the least sign of weakness or provocation. He guarded his poppy fields to the death, but if he was sending men up into the highlands at night that meant U Than was all stirred up about something.

Bolan had a good idea what.

"Have you seen the woman?"

"No, but I saw crash site. It was no 'catastrophic mechanical failure.' That plane shot down. I know cannon hits when I see them."

"Any survivors?"

Nyin shook his head. "No one survive that. You want to see?"

"No, the woman is our priority, and according to intel she jumped right before the fighters opened up."

"What woman look like?"

Bolan tapped an icon on his screen and called up a photo of Lily Na. "This."

"God damn!" Nyin shook his head in wonder. "That worth going to war over!"

Bolan changed the screen back to the GPS tracking Lily's transponder signal and then spoke over his link. "Base, this is Striker. Have established contact with Fat Man. Proceeding to signal source."

"Copy that, Striker."

Bolan turned to Nyin. "You ready to go to war?"

Nyin grinned and brandished an ancient-looking .30 carbine. "Always!"

"Then follow me." Bolan set out at a ground-eating jog, and despite his laughing-Buddha-like physique Nyin kept up easily. Bolan watched as the signal got closer and closer on his screen. They had to stop twice as armed men passed by on the trails through the heavy woods.

"Dangerous place," Nyin muttered after a group of men passed by. The men weren't wearing uniforms and wore a hodge-podge of Western and traditional highland clothing. They also carried a collection of weapons from the latest assault rifles to World War II relics. All carried one or more blades. They were sweeping the forest trails and keeping a wary eye on the forest itself. Traditionally it was where danger came from. They were right to be wary. This night Mack Bolan crouched among the giant ferns, and the forest had never been more dangerous.

Bolan and Nyin moved out and quickly came to a river. They dropped low by its banks and observed. A village huddled on either side of the river. The lights in the village were all out. On a low hill above the village sat what could only be described as a fortress. The main house was low, sprawling and made of heavy wooden beams and roofed with tile. A number of similarly constructed smaller outbuildings squatted around it like satellites. A bamboo palisade topped with razor wire surrounded the entire complex, and a twenty-foot-tall guard tower that had a good vantage on the village below completed security.

Bolan was pretty sure he knew the answer, but he asked anyway. "What is this place?"

Nyin pointed toward the collection of huts huddling together by the river. "That is Ta village." He peered unhappily at the fortress on the hill. "That is house of U Than." Nyin chewed on his lip pensively. He seemed to know the answer, but asked anyway, as well. "You have located girl?"

Bolan nodded as he stared at his screen and noted the distance between himself and the transponder signal. He looked up at the house of U Than. "She's in there."

3

The village was in lockdown. U Than's place was lit up like a Christmas tree, but the village was dark and nothing moved. The only activity was a pair of armed men who stood on the little bamboo pier smoking cigarettes, clearly bored with guard duty.

Bolan and Nyin made their approach through the tiny, muddy lanes between the huts. Most of the huts were up on low stilts, and beneath them pigs grunted in their pens and an occasional chicken squawked. In the distance, a water buffalo lowed in its enclosure. Bolan and Nyin moved past canoes up on racks and fishing nets hanging to dry from posts.

At five yards Bolan drew his blades.

He lunged as one of the sentries turned to spit betel juice into the river. The man went limp as the tomahawk head crunched into the top of his skull. The second sentry's cigarette sagged in his mouth in shock. Before he could do anything other than stare, Nyin's *dha* flashed from its sheath with alacrity that would have given a Japanese samurai pause. The sentry's head came a few tendons short from flying off his neck. Bolan thought rumors about Nyin doing some headhunting with the Naga tribes might not be entirely scurrilous. Bone splintered as Bolan retrieved his tomahawk. Nyin took a moment to relieve the dead gangsters of their money, betel and cigarettes, and then he and Bolan slid the two corpses into the river and washed the blood from their blades. Nyin shoved a leaf-wrapped quid of betel into his mouth and offered the pouch to Bolan.

The soldier shook his head. "I'm trying to give it up."

Nyin grinned and resheathed his blade. "Well, we have conquered Ta village."

So they had. "Fort U Than may be a little harder."

"Maybe," Nyin agreed.

Bolan climbed to the top of the open, A-frame canoe shelter and turned his binoculars on U Than's domicile. Nyin perched next to him and pulled out his own binoculars. Bolan scanned the grounds and stopped as he came to the wide porch leading to the main house. Most Burmese barely cracked five feet tall, and most of the guards' assault rifles seemed almost as large as they were. The four men up on the porch were all pushing six feet, were heavily tattooed and had the physiques of gladiators. "Those men on the porch. U Than's personal bodyguard?"

"Mmm," Nyin grunted. "Thai kickboxers. Leg breakers. Bad men."

U Than seemed to be recruiting from the heavyweight division. An even larger man came out on the porch. His head was shaved, and his ears were cauliflowered masses hanging from his head. The man's eyebrows appeared to be mostly scar tissue. He appeared to be several inches taller than Bolan and perhaps half again as heavy. Thrust in his sash was a Colt .45, and the hilt of a *dha* twice as large as Nyin's stuck up over his left shoulder. "Who's the gorilla?"

"That is Maung. Very bad man."

Maung gave off the unmistakable air of command. "U Than's number two?"

"Yes."

Bolan sighed. "Rescue missions…"

Nyin cocked his head. "What?"

"Nothing." Bolan put away his binoculars and slid off the roof of the canoe shed. "Let's do this."

"How?" Nyin hopped down. "Place locked up tight."

Bolan glanced at the dark, dappled waters of the river. It flowed down around the hill, and U Than had some canoes and speedboats tied up on a bamboo pier of his own. "Can you swim?"

"No." Nyin stared at the river in horror. "And there are crocodiles."

Bolan glanced behind him at the village canoes. The men in the guard tower would undoubtedly see them long before they got to the pier. "I guess we do it the hard way."

"You will want a diversion."

Bolan smiled. "Yeah, I'm gonna want a diversion. You know what to do with an M-203?"

Nyin was a small man with teeth that belonged in the mouth of a horse rather than a human, and he showed them. "As private, I was grenadier in my squad."

"Good." Bolan handed Nyin his rifle and pulled three grenades from his bandolier. "This one is offensive, high explosive, big boom. When I give you the signal, I'm going to want you to lob it into the compound. That's when I'll use flexible charge to cut through the palisade. The second one is tear gas, which will keep everyone occupied and intrigued while I make my insertion into the big house. Number three is white phosphorus. When I send you the signal, I want you to light up U Than's cottage like a torch."

Nyin's smile threatened to give away their position. "I light 'em up good!"

"I'll be coming out fast. Plan A is that I steal a speedboat and pick you up. Failing that, I want you to put a Willy Pete into U Than's boat dock, and I'll meet you back on the promontory where we first met. If it goes to hell, just get out. You have a cell phone?"

"Yes. Unfortunately battery is low."

Bolan pulled a phone from his web gear. "Take mine." Bolan tapped the motherboard strapped to his forearm. "I can call you with this. Give me thirty minutes to get to the far side of the palisade."

Nyin put a hand on Bolan's shoulder. "It is not a bad plan. I am honored to fight with you."

Bolan clapped him on the shoulder. "You just keep your head up, your ass down and your eyes open. Like I said, I'll be coming back fast."

"I will await your signal."

Bolan moved back through the village lanes. He could hear people murmuring within the huts, but no one opened a shutter or peered down. The Ta villagers had long ago learned not to be too curious about what went on in their valley late at night. Bolan jogged back into the rain forest and took a game trail that circled wide around U Than's castle. Once again, he had to pull a fade into the towering hardwoods as a patrol of gangsters came by. The good news was they were patrolling the wrong way. Bolan moved around to the back of the compound. He cut a length of flexible charge from his knapsack and a hoop just big enough to crawl through. He exposed the adhesive strip, pushed in a detonator pin and pressed the hoop into the bamboo. Bolan threaded a suppressor tube onto the muzzle of his machine pistol and text-messaged Nyin.

"Do it."

The M-203 thumped down in the village.

Bolan put his finger on the detonator button and counted down the seconds. The compound lit up in an orange flash as the offensive grenade detonated. Bolan pressed his own detonator, and the crack of the flexible charge was lost in the thunder. Armed men spilled out of the main house like a kicked-over anthill. The tear-gas grenade landed, and its multiple skip-chaser bomblets broke apart and began spewing out gray gas. The two men in the watchtower were shouting and pointing frantically. The men below began flailing and clawing at their eyes as what they thought was smoke from the explosion turned out to be war-strength CN tear gas.

Bolan pushed in the panel of bamboo he'd cut with his charge and crawled into the compound. Everyone was running toward the commotion while Bolan moved toward the back of the main house. The back of the fortress was more prosaic than the front and marked by pig enclosures, outdoor barbecue pits large enough to roast entire hogs and heat woks large enough for a grown man to go sledding in. Bolan moved through laundry lines hung with Western clothes, as well as native sarongs and tunics. He dropped between two stone washbasins as the back door flew open and a pair of men with submachine guns checked the back perimeter. Bolan waited a moment to be sure no one was behind them, then rose up with the 93-R in both hands. The machine pistol barely whispered as he put a 3-round burst into each man's chest. Bolan moved up the low stone steps past the two dead men and entered U Than's compound.

The back porch opened onto the kitchen. A pair of women wearing turbans were huddled in a corner clutching each other as gunfire rattled from the front of the compound. They stared in slack-jawed horror at the grease-painted, camouflaged giant who had appeared in their midst. Bolan put a finger to his lips, and the two women nodded in vigorous assent. One of the women had a bruise under her eye, and Bolan suspected U Than and the boys weren't too respectful of the hired help. They cringed as Bolan loomed over them and tried to press themselves back through the wall as he dropped to a knee in front of them. Their fear turned to awe as Bolan displayed Lily's photo on the PDA on his wrist. He reached into a pocket of web gear and produced two thick folds of Burmese currency. He held the money up and shrugged. "Where?" he asked quietly.

Both women pointed back the way Bolan had come.

Bolan cleared the screen on his PDA and brought up the sketching function. He took out the stylus and drew a quick sketch with a circle for the palisade and squares for the main house and the outbuildings. Bolan shrugged again.

Both women pointed at the smaller square directly behind the main house.

Bolan handed them the money and retraced his steps. His target was the largest of the outbuildings. It was a heavy-beamed A-frame with bamboo for walls, and the smell of smoked meat and fish radiated out from it. The Burmese people were overwhelmingly Theravada Buddhists, but most were also confirmed carnivores. Bolan's destination was the meat-smoking and slaughterhouse. There was a light on within it.

Bolan crept to the door. It wasn't particularly well fitted, and through the seams he could see it was barred from the inside. He could also hear voices within. Bolan cut a two-inch length of flexible charge and pressed it into the doorjamb. The charge hissed as he pressed the detonator, and the shaped charged burned through the bar. The soldier put his boot into the door, and it flung open on its leather hinges.

Two men started up in shock from playing with a laptop and reached for their automatic rifles. Bolan nailed both men in the chest with a triburst each, and they dropped to the dirt floor. Lily Na hung two feet from the floor in a bamboo tiger cage. Only sweat and humidity kept the shredded remnants of her black cocktail dress clinging to a divinely curved body. She had a black eye, but she perked the eyebrow over her good one in interest as she took in the commando before her and managed a smirk. "Hey, sailor."

Bolan shook his head at her situation. "This U Than asshole comes straight out of a comic book."

"He has issues." Lily shrugged. "No doubt."

"Miss Na, my name is Cooper. I'm here to rescue you." Bolan took in the tiger cage. It was made of bamboo, but the shafts were as thick as his arm and the knots of hemp that bound it together were like fists. A heavy iron padlock bound the door shut. He had only a foot of flexible charge left, and trying to saw or hack his way through any part of it would take too much time. Bolan handed Lily his pistol and pulled his lock-pick case from a pouch in his web gear. He chose a pair of tensile steel picks, put his tactical light between his teeth and began working the lock.

Lily spoke low. "Men are coming."

Bolan ignored her and repeated the breaking-and-entering mantra. "Forget everything else, work the lock."

"They are almost here," she urged.

Bolan worked the lock.

"They are upon us."

Bolan didn't speak Burmese, but he understood the snarl of command coming from the open door. Lily spoke in a whisper. "Maung is here with two of his men. They are telling me to drop my gun and you to freeze."

"Do it," Bolan ordered.

Maung shouted in broken English. "You! Drop gun!"

"But—"

"Do it!"

The Beretta fell through the floor of the cage. Bolan sighed inwardly as the weapon dropped into the blood-catching cistern set in the floor. A voice shouted the same angry words in Burmese twice. Lily flinched. "He says turn—"

"You! Turn round!" Maung snarled.

Bolan turned slowly.

Maung was flanked by a pair of U Than's kickboxers. All three carried licensed copies of Uzi submachine guns. Bolan dropped the lock picks. Maung motioned at the tactical light between the Executioner's teeth. He very slowly removed it.

Maung smiled to reveal his gold teeth in triumph.

Bolan spun the bezel in the buttcap with his thumb, and the flashlight went to full-strength-strobe mode. Most tactical lights had an output of eighty to one hundred lumens. Bolan's Farm-modified light sprayed out at a thousand and blinked at over twenty times per second. It would burn up his battery in moments, but light strobing at that intensity was known to induce seizures in epileptics, and during tests even trained soldiers and martial artists lost their spatial orientation and were reduced to staggering like blind drunks.

The man to Maung's right took a step forward and fell to his hands and knees. The man to Maung's left teetered and stumbled against the doorjamb. Maung stood like a man leaning into a high wind and sprayed off a blind burst with his weapon. Lily yelped and cringed as bullets tore splinters from her bamboo cage.

Bolan strode forward strobing continuously. The massive amping up of the light's candlepower wasn't the only modification. The body of the flashlight was titanium, and the rim surrounding the lens sported teeth like the jaws of a bear trap for impact fighting. Bolan drove the still strobing light between Maung's eyes like an ice pick.

Maung's septum disintegrated beneath the blow. The shock of it dropped him to the floor as limp as a fish. Bolan drove his boot up between the legs of the man leaning against the door, and he fell vomiting next to his kneeling comrade. His comrade's jaw shattered beneath Bolan's heel. The big American drew his tomahawk and began chopping furiously at the hemp bindings of the cage. It was like chopping wood, but the strands slowly came apart. Bolan grabbed the bars of the cage and ripped the door off its hinges.

Lily hopped down and grabbed her laptop.

Bolan scooped up a fallen weapon and checked the loads. "That's it?"

Lily closed the laptop and picked up a fallen Uzi. "Yes, they did not know what they had. They were using it to peruse pornography."

"Let's get you out of here." Bolan and Lily ran from the smokehouse.

The soldier snatched a sarong and a man's shirt from the clothesline in passing as they ran for the hole burned in the wall. The men in the guard tower were pointing and screaming, but no one on the ground and in the gas was paying them any attention.

Bolan spoke into his phone. "Fatso, hit the tower, then fire the house."

"I have bad guys coming my way!" Nyin responded, but the grenade launcher down in Ta village thumped. The two men up in the tower noticed Bolan and Lily as they reached the palisade. One began shouting, while the other raised a rifle.

The grenade launcher thumped again as Lily wriggled through the hole. The Willy Pete hit the front of the house, and the men on the porch screamed as white-hot smoke and streamers of burning metal erupted in all directions. Bolan slid outside. Men continued to stream out the gate, and at the pier engines were roaring into life as armed men piled into the boats for an amphibious assault on the grenadier in the village.

Bolan spoke into his motherboard. "Fatso, I'm not going to be able to reach the boats. Extract, and I'll meet you at the promontory."

"Yes, Coop!" Nyin responded. "I am extracting!"

Bolan grabbed Lily's hand and ran for the tree line. Behind

them gray gas and white smoke was blanketing U Than's fortress
in a fog of war. It was a war that had just begun, and tomorrow
it would become a hunt. U Than was going to want some payback.

   It was more than five hundred miles to the border of Thailand.

4

Ta village

Captain Tam-Sam Dai passed out small bribes and iron-palmed slaps liberally among the villagers. None seemed to be able to give him any useful information, and he doubted hard interrogation would yield anything more. U Than had kept the village locked down for two days after salvaging everything of value from the crashed jet and capturing the woman. The villagers had heard the fighting the previous night and had quite prudently locked their shutters and doors and huddled in their huts with the lights off.

Dai was a member of the PRC's Special Operations Forces, specifically their highly secretive Special Purpose Force, or infiltration unit. The PRC kept special forces units whose members could pass as citizens of every nation they had a common border with, as well as many they did not. Dai was a member of China's ethnic Shan minority. His skin was copper colored, and though incredibly broad shouldered he stood barely five feet tall. He spoke perfect Burmese and could easily pass himself as a native hill man of Burma, Thailand or Laos.

Chinese military satellites had been intensely scrutinizing the area of the crash site. Dai and his team had been dropped in immediately but found the wreckage and the bodies stripped of all valuables. The satellites had detected the battle last night and vectored Dai and his men in. Dai had captured a villager, given him an envelope with a very thick stack of Chinese one-hundred yuan notes to take to U Than, along with the message that he would like to meet with him.

The meeting had gone well. Several million yuan had soothed U Than's troubled soul. Promise of aid in rebuilding had further convinced the warlord that he should conduct business with the Chinese triads rather than the syndicates in Thailand. All very profitable. Captain Dai's superiors in Beijing had already commended him on it; however, the loyalties of U Than were not the main issue here.

Dai glanced up as Sergeant Hwa-Che came trotting down from the burned-out mansion and gave his report. He, too, was Shan but he gave his report in Mandarin so that U Than and his people would not know what was said. "Captain, we have discovered residue of high explosive in the tower top and in the crater in the compound. The house was clearly burned down with white phosphorous. The hole in the palisade was cut with flexible charge. I believe the grenade barrage was done from Ta village and acted as a diversion while the Na woman and the computer were extracted." The sergeant spit betel and frowned mightily. "It is clearly the work of U.S. Special Forces."

Captain Dai had already surmised that. He frowned at Hwa-Che. He knew the sergeant's ways well. "What is bothering you?"

Hwa-Che slid his eye over to the pier where U Than and several of his men were gathered by the boats. "I have spoken with Maung."

Dai was an adept at snake-hand kung fu, but even he had to admit the hulking man gave him pause. "And what says the mighty Maung?"

"He says there was only one American."

Dai scowled. "One?"

"Yes, and have you noticed Maung's face, Captain?"

It was hard not to. Maung was incredibly ugly to begin with, but now both of his eyes were a raccoon's mask of bruising and his shattered nose looked like a flattened squid. "Yes, I have noticed."

"He said the American did it. Maung and two of the Thai bullyboys had the drop on the American, yet he defeated them with a flashlight and his bare hands and then took the woman. One has a broken jaw and the other sits on a sack of ice and pees blood."

Dai's scowl deepened. "I find that hard to believe."

"I have also spoken with our Naga trackers. There are only one pair of boot prints leading to and away from the compound, and leading away the bare feet of a single woman."

"What about here in the village?"

Hwa-Che shrugged. "All the footprints in Ta village are bare feet or native sandals. On the other hand, the Naga say the boot prints in the compound are large, definitely Caucasian, and undoubtedly belonging to a man such as Maung has described."

Dai settled on his plan. "Have the Naga begin tracking immediately. Gather the men and any of U Than's who seem likely, and tell U Than he will be well rewarded for any assistance he gives us."

"What is the plan, Captain?"

"One or two Americans, operating alone, could play hide-and-seek with us for months up here in the mountains, but that is not their mission. They must try to break out of Burma."

Hwa-Che brightened as he saw it. "The woman!"

"Yes, the woman is the key. She is not American Special Forces. She is Taiwanese intelligence. Whoring, spying and assassination are her game. She will slow her rescuers."

One look at the woman had convinced U Than there was a hefty ransom somewhere, and he had kept his men from abusing the woman. Captain Dai had told U Than over the phone as he came in that China wanted the woman intact. That was not out of any sense of propriety. Lily Na would be horribly punished, but Chinese interrogators would start the punishment, and they did not feel like swimming in dirty water. Dai's men had all seen her picture and been briefed on the mission. They were already gambling numbers for who would take her first. Dai did not discourage such talk. Their only orders concerning her were to bring her back alive and ready for interrogation. As captain, he would of course get first dibs.

Dai peered up into the thickly wooded hills. "We will run them down."

FOR A WOMAN who had spent two days lost in the mountains and twenty-four hours as the guest of an opium lord hanging in a cage, Bolan thought Lily looked fantastic. She had cut the flowered batik-print sarong Bolan had stolen for her to above the knees for action and knotted the men's dress shirt under her ribs. She carried her Uzi with familiar ease.

But her feet were bruised, abraded and swollen. She had been barefoot for forty-eight hours in the mountains, and their night run from U Than's compound hadn't done her any favors. By the end of another day of hiking, her feet would be broken open, bleeding and going septic in the Southeast Asian soil and Bolan would be carrying her.

Lily sat against a tree and wiggled her swollen toes. "So what is our plan for extraction?"

"That's a good question," Bolan replied. "Burma is shaped like a diamond, and we're in the north. We've got six hundred miles of Chinese border to the east, and then about the same to the west with India."

Her jade eyes narrowed slightly. "India is in play?"

"It looks that way, and they may not be our friends on this one. I have forged documents for both of us and money. There are two airports in the north, Seniku and Bhamo. Both are about equidistant to us. We could clean ourselves up and pretend to be tourists, or just try bribing our way onto a plane. Then again we have to assume Chinese and Indian intelligence will be watching all the airports, and you and I are going to stand out in a crowd. For that matter, Burma just had a plane shot down over her airspace and we have to assume security is on high alert nationwide. We have to assume Chinese intelligence will be informing key operatives and informants to be on the lookout for us."

Lily's lips quirked slightly. "So, the Thai border."

"Yeah," Bolan agreed. "If we can get close enough to it, the U.S. and several of her allies have the assets to send in an extraction team for us, or if worse comes to worst we can just walk across it. We could also head southeast for the coast and arrange a submarine extraction. That's about the same distance."

The woman looked at her feet. "Five hundred miles either way, and almost all of it mountains."

"Like I said, you and I stick out. It's best if we stay off the roads and out of the towns. We can try stealing a car or truck and let Nyin drive, or do the same with a boat down one of the major rivers, but military checkpoints are frequent."

"So we walk."

"Yeah, it looks like we'll have to hoof it most of the way and let Nyin go into the villages and towns along the way for supplies."

Lily nodded, steeling herself for what lay ahead. "Then he had better go shoe shopping for me, and fast."

Nyin gazed at her feet for a moment and then squatted on his heels before her. He began rummaging through the old canvas gas-mask bag he carried. He pulled out a little brown bottle and smiled triumphantly. Bolan smiled, as well. "Chinese medicated wine?"

Nyin almost lost his smile. "*Burmese* stone-fist liniment."

Lily sagged against the trunk of the tree with a blissful sigh as Nyin went to work rubbing the liniment into her feet.

"How are you otherwise?" Bolan asked.

"I am all right."

Bolan eyed the woman critically. "They didn't hurt you?"

Her jade-green eyes went as cold as stone. "Nothing was done to me that has not been done before." She sighed again as Nyin went to work on her toes. "And nothing so pleasant as this." She gave Bolan a small smile. "I will pull my own weight."

Bolan had to give it to her. The woman from Taipei was tough. "Fair enough." He dropped to one knee beside her and picked up the remnants of her silk cocktail dress. He cut four two-inch-wide, bandagelike strips from around the hem. Nyin finished his medicated massage, and Bolan took the strips and cross-wound them from Lily's toes to her calves and tied them off. The woman eyed her shimmering new footwear. "You know, there are people in Mongolia who still wear these instead of socks."

"Siberia, too." Bolan nodded at his handiwork. "Silk, twice the tensile strength of steel." He stuffed the rest of the shredded dress into his knapsack. There might be more uses for it yet. Bolan held out his hand. "Let's get you up." He pulled the woman up. She took a few gingerly steps and then rose up on her toes several times like a ballerina.

"I can walk."

"Good." Bolan checked his GPS. They hadn't established much distance from U Than's place, and he suspected all too soon Lily was going to have to run.

5

"We got trackers, boss." Nyin came up puffing from the trail behind them.

Bolan took a pull from his canteen and offered it to Nyin. "How far back?"

"About three kilometers." Nyin took a long drink and pointed back. "You should be able to see them in a minute or two when they top that rise."

Bolan took out his binoculars and waited, giving Lily some time to breathe. Men came over the ridge just as Nyin had said. The men were small, bare chested but wearing sarongs and turbans. The men's arms, thighs and chests were heavily tattooed. Each man carried an M-16 rifle and thrust through his sash was a short, heavy ax with a triangular blade. The hilts were tufted with masses of red-and-black hair. "Naga?"

"That's right, Hot rod, and those good old boy. From way up-country." Nyin patted the hilt of his sword. "This *dha,* it made for war. Those axes *dao,* they made for taking head. You saw tails on handle?"

"I saw them."

"*Dao* made for tourists? Tails made of goat hair, very long, very pretty, like tail of horse or hair of pretty girl. Hair on those axes short. Most likely human. Those men expert hunter. Expert tracker. Never tire." Nyin's perennial smile stayed on his face, but he shook his head. "We in trouble."

"Can you talk to them?"

Nyin chewed his lower lip. "Don't know. Have to get close

to find out. Not sure I want to get that close. Could be unhealthy. Wrong tribe? Even adopted, I still traditional enemy."

"What about bribing them?"

"Don't know. I tell you this. No Naga around here friend of U Than. U Than clean out local hills for agriculture, if you know what I mean. Make lowlander do work for him. U Than not wanting any hillbilly around."

That was interesting. "You're saying U Than didn't hire them?"

"Nyin saying any man U Than send up into Naga country to hire them not come back." The Burmese eyed Bolan shrewdly. "Nyin saying that maybe whoever hire them can outbid you."

Nyin was probably right. He had some very thick wads of bills in his money belt, but Bolan was pretty sure the People's Republic of China could outbid him at the moment. "Then we'll have to discourage them."

"That something Nyin would like to see."

"Well, you're going to." Bolan handed Nyin his laser range-finding binoculars. "You're ranging me."

"Ah!" Nyin took the optics reverently.

Bolan handed Lily his canteen. "Nyin and I are going to do some discouragement duty. Why don't you rest here for a bit? Nyin, leave her the phone I gave you, just in case."

Nyin handed over the phone and then rummaged through his mess bag. He pulled out the little brown medicine bottle. "Reapply."

Lily didn't argue. She took the canteen, phone and the medicine bottle and sat down with obvious relief. Bolan and Nyin went back down the game trail. Coming down from the escarpment, a ledge broke the rows of hardwoods marching up the hillsides. "There. They should be there in about five minutes if they keep the pace."

Nyin grunted in agreement.

Along the trail, it was about two and half kilometers to the cliff, but from hillside to hillside it was around five hundred meters. Far out of range for most assault rifles without an optic sight. Bolan dropped into a rifleman's squat. Nyin brought the laser range-finding binoculars to his eyes and pressed the laser designator button. Invisible to the human eye, the binoculars sent out a beam and measured precisely where it stopped. "Five hundred twenty-five meters."

The scout rifle was not a sniper weapon. Rather it was made for rapid sharp-shooting at close to medium ranges. Nevertheless, the Austrian engineering of the rifle was precise in the extreme. It was as accurate as the man shooting it and could reach out and touch Fort Mudge if the man behind it was good enough. Bolan wrapped his rifle sling tight around his left arm and dropped his elbow to his knee, wedging himself into a solid firing platform.

Nyin spoke quietly. "I see them. They come."

Bolan kept his eyes on the open cliff. "Give me a count."

Nyin was quiet for a moment. "Three…two…one…"

The lead man came out across the cliff at a steady jog. Bolan's rifle was suppressed, and to keep it quiet the bullets it fired were heavy and subsonic. The Executioner put his crosshairs on the lead Naga's chest and then gave him three degrees of lead. Bolan took up slack on the trigger as he tracked the running man.

The rifle bucked back against the big American's shoulder. Bolan instantly worked his bolt. In the split second it took him to chamber a fresh round, the man ran another two meters and then suddenly his head broke apart like a melon. His rifle and ax flew in two directions as his arms flapped like a ruptured pigeon. His forward momentum dropped him into an ugly sprawl onto the escarpment.

The other three Naga instantly disappeared into the trees.

Nyin whistled softly and lowered his binoculars. "I am in awe of you."

Bolan picked up his spent brass shell and shrugged. "I was aiming for his chest."

Nevertheless, Bolan suspected the message had been delivered. He retrieved his binoculars from Nyin and flipped on camera mode. "Get Lily moving. I'll catch up."

CAPTAIN DAI STARED at the headless corpse from a prudent distance. He was having a hard time believing that one man was a sniper, grenadier and an infiltrator. "Where are the Naga?"

Hwa-Che sighed. "Hiding."

Dai searched the heavens for strength. The blue skies of Yunnan Province seemed a million miles away, and the gods of his fathers seemed to have abandoned him in this place. Naga were a warrior people, but they hardly ever engaged in open war. Headhunting was more like a lifelong, lethal game of tag, and Naga could hide for days while waiting for their prey to pass by. Or their angry employers to go away. "Tell them double pay. In gold."

Sergeant Hwa-Che raised his voice to parade-ground decibels and shouted the words in Naga. The three remaining trackers seemed to sprout out of the forest eagerly holding out their hands. Hwa-Che grimaced in distaste and crossed the Naga's palms with Chinese golden panda coins.

Dai turned back to his team. "Private Su!"

Private Su did not look up from scanning the opposite hillside with the powered telescope of his JS sniper rifle. "If the American is still there, he is very well hidden."

Dai nodded. "Old Man! Give us cover and check the body for booby traps!"

Corporal "Old Man" Cao was the team's grandfather. He was pushing field retirement and was a long veteran of China's mis-behaviors on the Vietnamese border. He did his best work with a knife and was an inveterate lurker. He was a head taller than everyone else in the team, blade thin, and assiduously cultivated his wispy mustache and beard. Cao pulled a pair of smoke grenades and hurled them out onto the escarpment. Thick white smoke began occluding the cliff and a good bit of the hillside. Cao ran out and disappeared into the smoke. He quickly came back grinning and holding up a ghoulish prize. "No traps, Captain. But I found this." Cao handed Dai a bloody bullet. "Do you see? American .308. But heavy. Round nose rather than pointed. The American fired through a silencer. That is why we did not hear the shot."

"And you think the enemy having a silenced sniper rifle is good news?"

"No, Captain." Cao continued smiling. "But in a sniper

battle, Private Su will outrange him by three hundred meters. Perhaps four."

Private Su smiled without looking up from his optic. "I believe the corporal is correct, and further I do not believe the American has a real sniper rifle. It would not be appropriate to his mission. I just think he is a very good shot."

Dai looked back and forth between his two grinning men. "And if the American is clever enough to have brought along a few full-powered shells?"

"Full-power ammunition will destroy his silencer, and lose him the one real advantage he has," Cao concluded smugly. "Any offensive action he takes now will be a terrible choice of alternatives, all fraught with danger."

Special forces operators were the same the world over. Even in the most regimented armies they knew they were better than everybody else, and discipline within the ranks became somewhat lax. Officers throughout China's two-million-man army could expect blind obedience out of their soldiers. In the special forces, respect had to be earned, and rise in rank came on ability and merit far more often than party and family connections or bribery. Dai did not reprimand his men for speaking out of turn. Private Su was one of the best shots to ever come out army sniper school, and Old Man Cao was a decorated veteran whose tactical opinion was worth its weight in gold.

"Sergeant, get the Naga moving. Corporal Cao, get the men across the escarpment before the smoke thins. We have hunting to do."

BOLAN LOWERED his binoculars. It wasn't good. Physically, it was hard to distinguish the Chinese from the Burmese auxiliaries, but since they were on a combat mission rather than infiltrating enemy territory they displayed it in the superior air they showed their flunkies, as well as their superior armament. That they weren't even trying to hide. They had the latest PRC and Russian equipment. Two men had backpacks with very suspicious looking, large-diameter tubes sticking up out of them.

Bolan counted at least one sniper among them, and he had been debating taking the shot on the man here and now when the enemy had popped smoke and begun moving. Bolan counted a twelve-man Chinese team, backed up by Maung and another fifteen of U Than's goons, as well the three remaining trackers.

Bolan worked his way back up the hillside and began loping down the trail. He quickly caught up with Nyin and Lily. The Taiwanese intelligence agent wasn't limping, but she was obviously in pain. "How're you doing?"

Lily kept her eyes on the ground ahead, keeping an eye out for rocks and trotting on soft soil. It was saving her pain, but she was also leaving very clear footprints. "I was supposed to be on a beach in Costa Rica by now." Her green eyes lifted for a moment and stared into the middle distance. "I am told the sand is pink."

"It is. Don't worry, we'll get your toes in the sand and piña colada in hand yet."

Lily smiled wanly and returned her gaze to the trail. "The thought of it is the only thing that keeps me moving."

Nyin was puffing along, but his smile stayed painted on. "How many?"

"Call it half a platoon. Maung and U Than's men I could probably cut up and scatter, but the Chinese team is going to give them backbone and prop it up with hard cash. They also have light support weapons and a sniper. They outrange everything we've got."

"What we do?"

"I was hoping you might have an idea."

Nyin pointed toward a range of hills to the southeast and laid out a plan as they ran. Bolan felt a headache coming on.

It wasn't necessarily a bad plan.

But it sure as hell wasn't good.

And unfortunately Bolan couldn't think of a better one.

6

Lily was clearly appalled. "This is not a good plan." She had to draw her knees to hip height with each sucking step she took through the abandoned paddy. Normally wet-rice farmers also farmed ducks and crayfish in the same fields, and between them they kept the fields fertilized and free of pests. Leeches covered Lily's bare legs, and the biting flies fearlessly buzzed through the blighted, overgrown rice plants and weeds and drew blood at an eye blink of inattention. Bolan had no attention to spare for the parasites.

They were literally walking through a minefield. Bolan mucked through the knee-deep swamp an inch at a time, using a five-foot pointed stick for a probe.

The problem for the Burmese military was that up in the highlands, with just a little bit of warning, rebels could melt away into the forests before an attack. However, almost all the rebels were farmers, and sooner or later they returned to their villages once the soldiers left. Like a number of governments, ruling junta had figured out there were few better ways to sow apprehension and dissension among farmers than to sow their fields with land mines. After the first few men and water buffalo lost their legs, the fields were abandoned and without a crop, so were the villages. Rebel strongholds became ghost towns, and the rebels and their families became masses of starving, migrant refugees. The Burmese army's weapon of choice was a locally produced copy of the U.S. M-14 antipersonnel mine. It carried just enough explosive to take a man's leg off at the knee, and was nicknamed the "toe-popper" for fairly obvious reasons.

So far, Bolan had found three of them.

Ostensibly the Burmese military kept charts of the minefields so that someday they could come and reclaim the farmland. Nyin, through various means, had acquired maps charting a number of the minefields in his area of operation. However, wet-rice farming was dependent on controlled flooding, and after a year or two without anyone manning the dykes the river had assumed its natural course.

Things had shifted a bit.

"They come soon!" Nyin stated.

Bolan moved inch by inch through the muck and worked his probe while ignoring mosquitoes the size of ballpoint pens that probed every inch of his exposed flesh and completely ignored the insect repellent he'd applied earlier.

"Soon!" Nyin grinned. His gleaming, sweaty head and bare arms seemed impervious to local insects. "Very soon!"

Bolan was trying to concentrate on the swamp in front of him. "Nyin, best for you to be quiet now."

Nyin ignored the sage advice. "Should be one right in front of you, Sex machine. One meter or less."

Bolan moved his stick softly through the muck like a plow until he encountered something hard. He probed the object softly. A toe-popper was about the size of a can of chewing tobacco. This one was about the size of a half-gallon can of paint. Bolan very gently touched the top and found the little fusing tower that held the three sensor pins. It was a mine known as a Bouncing Betty. When the sensor pins were disturbed, a charge in the bottom of the mine would literally make the mine jump three to four feet in the air before a pound of C-4 high explosive detonated. The prefragmented metal liner filled with steel ball bearings was lethal within five meters and would badly shred anyone within twenty-seven meters. It also had a pin in the side that could be set with a trip wire, and Bolan spent a few moments gingerly probing for it. It gave him an idea. "Give me the spare stick."

Nyin handed him the stick, and Bolan broke it in two and care-fully stuck a piece of stick against either side of the mine so that the tips just barely protruded out of the water. Bolan moved on, painstakingly clearing another fifty feet, inch by inch. After what seemed like hours, the muck reluctantly released him as he hauled himself up the embankment. He pulled up Nyin and Lily and they flopped exhausted among the weeds. Bolan grabbed his binoculars and scanned the hillside on the other side of the field. They were clear for the moment. He rose to his feet and stared at the empty huts with their gaping, empty windows and doors. "Take Lily and keep moving. I'll catch up."

Nyin grunted and Lily sighed as they woodenly rose and moved through the ghost village. Bolan followed them until he found a decent hide in the shadows of a pig enclosure beneath a hut. It had a nice panoramic view of the field. He lay down in the dirt with his rifle and waited.

He didn't have to wait long.

The enemy deployed down the hillside in a skirmish line with the Naga following Bolan and his team's spoor as easily as bloodhounds. The Chinese had a dilemma. They did not know whether Bolan and his team had gone all the way across the field or turned midstream and followed the river. Three men, clearly soldiers, cut themselves switches and took one of the Naga into the rice field with them. Bolan and his team had tried not to break any rice stalks or reeds, but in the end it had proved impossible. The Naga stood behind the three-man probing line and directed them like a pointer.

Bolan put his crosshairs on the two sticks and waited.

When they were within ten feet of the sticks, Bolan fired. The suppressed rifle made barely any noise at all beneath the hut and none at all discernible to those wading out in the paddy. The Naga nearly jumped out of his skin as a little geyser of water shot up in the air where the bullet hit. Bolan flicked his bolt, lowered his aim an inch and fired again.

The Bouncing Betty erupted out of the water like a beheaded jack-in-the-box and detonated with a sound like a giant door slamming. There was a puff of orange fire and a spasm of smoke. The Naga tracker and the three-man mine-clearing team rippled and twisted like wheat in a high wind as hundreds of steel ball bearings passed through their bodies. The sound of the explosion echoed against the hills. The dead men sank beneath the surface of the flooded field, leaving spreading red stains in the scummy green water.

Bolan watched as one of the men across the field consulted with another. One man was clearly the Chinese officer and the other his second in command. Bolan itched for the shot, but it was long and would let everyone know he was in the village. He waited while they talked and let himself breathe a sigh of relief as the Chinese team broke into two groups, each with one of the remaining trackers, and began moving north and south down each end of the valley. They were going to go around and waste valuable time trying to pick up Bolan's tracks again.

The big American crawled backward and kept the hut between himself and the other side of the valley. He hadn't seen the sniper, but Bolan could feel the killer scanning for him through his scope. Bolan stopped on a little landing of the stairs that led up to the stilted hut and did a little shopping. He faded back and, when he reached the trees, he broke into a run.

It was time to do some distance.

SERGEANT HWA-CHE WAS GONE. Captain Dai couldn't believe it. The man who had taught him everything he knew and recommended him to officer candidate school was dead in a nameless, fly-ridden rice field. It was a peasant's death. The American had led them straight into it. It was almost inconceivable. Southeast Asia was their territory, their specialty, their turf, as the Americans would say. Dai looked down to see his hand was shaking. He had unconsciously opened it into the snake-fist formation. It shook with his need to reach into the American's chest, rip out his beating heart and show it to him.

Old Man Cao approached Dai wearily. "We are down to two trackers."

"I am aware of that, Corporal," Dai replied.

"However, it is confirmed. They are a party of only three. An American soldier, the Na woman and an unidentified third party, wearing native sandals. I suspect he is a native, probably a CIA intelligence asset."

Dai had his own sources. "I find that very hard to believe, Corporal."

Cao wiped sweat from his brow and shrugged. "Who else could it be, Captain?"

"Who would you suspect, Old Man?"

Cao draped his weapon across his shoulder. "We are the dominant outside intelligence force in Myanmar."

"Do you believe we are up against rogue Chinese agents?"

That was unthinkable. "Well, the Thais wield great influence as a trading partner, but we have thoroughly infiltrated their intelligence agencies."

"So tell me, Old Man, who could this thorn in our side be?"

Corporal Cao spit the words. *"Yang gui zi."*

"The foreign devil" could mean anyone unfortunate enough not to have been born Chinese, but in the old days the words referred to one nation in particular. A nation that had not just been a thorn in the side of the Middle Kingdom, but had held the knife across its throat. "Yes," Dai agreed, "the English."

The United Kingdom was a shadow of the mighty empire it once was, and the English lion paled in comparison to the might of the Chinese dragon, but the English were stubborn and meddlesome. They still had one of the best intelligence agencies in the world and, most importantly, were a staunch ally of the United States.

Dai gazed at Cao steadily. "And?"

Cao turned his gaze northward. "And I believe any assets the English have here in the north would be local and involved in drug interdiction. I suspect the Americans have called in a favor."

"Very good. I am promoting you to acting sergeant, promotion to be confirmed by the battalion commander upon our successful return to Beijing." Cao beamed delightedly. Dai made an effort to scowl. "Now give me the rest of your report and wipe that stupid smile off of your face. You look like a peasant."

Cao snapped to attention. "The trackers have relocated their trail.

The shooter was the American. He took a firing position beneath one of the huts and stayed to hold us off while the other two ran."

Dai had suspected that, but he'd had to check the entire circumference of the fields regardless. The American had known that, too, and he would be using it to put distance between them. Dai's snake-hand formation closed into a white-knuckled fist. He would take Lily Na while his men cheered him on. The Burmese bastard that was helping her would die staked out over a fire. As for the American... Dai snarled over his shoulder, "Corporal Khoay-Peng!"

Khoay-Peng snapped to attention. "Yes, Captain!"

"Do you have your needles with you?"

"Yes, Captain!" Corporal Khoay-Peng was the team medic, and an accomplished acupuncturist in both the little- and big-needle style. With skillful application he could relieve headaches, unlock muscles in spasm and cure any number of maladies. He knew the nerve meridians and energy channels of the body like the back of his hand. Khoay-Peng was also a master of the poison-needle tradition. The same skills that could bring the sick and injured back to health could also plunge a human being into an agonizing hell where they would regurgitate any knowledge they had to make the horror end. Dai had read after-action debriefings where the victims had likened the pain to having their living nerves drawn from their body and pulled through heated sand.

"The American will require field interrogation."

"Yes, Captain."

Dai turned away from the swamp that had swallowed Sergeant Hwa-Che's bones. "Big-needle style."

"Yes, Captain."

Dai turned to his communications specialist. "Private Po."

Po trotted forward. "Yes, Captain."

"Set up the secure line. I need to make a phone call."

BOLAN CAUGHT UP again far too quickly. Lily was sitting on a tree stump while Nyin puffed on a clove cigarette and then pressed the glowing tip into the gorged bodies of the leeches covering Lily's legs. She had more than a dozen bleeding circles on her thighs and calves. Nyin surveyed his handiwork and then rose rubbing his hands. "We heard explosion, Coop. How many you kill?"

"I got four. Pretty sure three were Chinese, one was a tracker."

"Good!" Nyin smiled. "Very good."

Bolan turned to Lily and held up three pairs of sandals he'd found in the village. "I went shopping for you."

Lily began sizing them against her feet. "I see I am reduced to peasant chic." She chose a pair that just about fit her feet while Bolan cut her dry pairs of silk sock-bandages. "Nyin, you have any more ideas?"

Nyin chewed his lip. "Yes. A little way southwest is northern Myanmar railhead at Myitkyina. We ride on top of train and can jump off any time, and Chinese don't know where we jump off. We lose them."

"How far?"

"We can't go in Myitkyina. Full of soldiers. We have to skirt city and then hop train. Say…twenty-five kilometers?"

Bolan clicked on his PDA. "Base, this is Striker."

Barbara Price instantly answered. "I have you, Striker."

"I need satellite recon and train schedules for every freighter heading out of Myitkyina." Bolan glanced up at the sun and calculated. It was almost fifteen and half miles exactly, and they would be losing the light in a few hours. "I'm going to be there in three hours."

"Copy that, Striker. Will have intel for you ASAP."

"Striker out." Bolan powered down everything on the motherboard except for the signal the Farm was tracking. He would have to change batteries soon. He only had two spare sets and he had almost drained the first within twenty-four hours.

Lily took a deep breath. "Twenty-five kilometers, cross-country, in three hours."

Bolan nodded. There was no way to sugarcoat it. "You're going to have to run."

"So I suspected." She sighed.

"I'm going to run you till you puke and then run you until you puke again. Then I'm going to carry you, and then Nyin is. Then we're going to switch. We have to make time. We have to catch a train. We need to leave the Chinese eating our dust."

Lily stood. "I am ready."

7

Tom Marchant frowned as his phone rang. He had not been expecting the call. He turned on his voice scrambler and picked up the phone. "Variance," he answered, using his code name.

Captain Dai spoke in Mandarin. "Variance, this is Tiger Fork."

"Go ahead, Tiger Fork."

"We have encountered unexpected resistance. We believe Miss Na and the American commando are receiving aid from local Western assets."

Marchant rolled his eyes but kept his tone professional. "Impossible. I would know of any CIA assets in play."

"We believe the American knows he has been compromised somewhere along the line. We believe perhaps he is receiving aid from MI-6."

Marchant quirked an eyebrow. "Interesting."

"We believe he must be a local MI-6 asset. The Ministry of State Security believes it is most likely to be a man involved in drug interdiction, probably in league with or under the aegis of Interpol. Can you be of assistance?"

"I believe I can. Though it will take me a little time. What is your situation now?"

Dai paused. "We have taken casualties. We are down to two trackers."

Marchant stared at the map of Burma on his computer. "Do you require local reinforcements?"

"We believe the mission can be accomplished with the present force level. The enemy is leaving a fairly clear trail and we are gaining. Give me an update on their current position."

Marchant poured himself two fingers of cognac and swirled the snifter as he watched the satellite stream on his computer. "They are currently 8.4 kilometers north of Myitkyina. Five kilometers south of your position. They are currently heading straight for the city, and slowing. They are paralleling the main road. I suggest you make all effort to run them down now. If they reach the city, they will have multiple venues of escape, refuge and perhaps even allies."

Dai clearly didn't like receiving suggestions. "We are making every effort."

Marchant made another suggestion. "Who is your fastest runner?"

"Despite his age, Sergeant Cao."

"You can't afford to put your team on the road and be spotted, but send Cao. Send him with just a pistol and knife and in native clothing. Have him run ahead into the city along the road. If you fail to overtake the American on the trail, I will vector Cao in to intercept."

Dai's silence was stony, but it was clear he didn't have a better idea. "I will dispatch Sergeant Cao immediately."

"I will contact you as soon as I have the information you requested. Variance out." Marchant killed the connection and gazed once more upon the map of Burma. He was surprised that the Chinese were having such problems with their quarry. Burma was practically their playground. English interference was an interesting gambit, but one he had a counter for. Marchant connected to another sat phone. An English-accent voice answered. "Hullo?"

Marchant spoke in English. "Morris, you dizzy bastard! How's it hanging?"

Hugh Morris was MI-6's head man in Southeast Asia, and he and Marchant had worked on some very successful operations together. "Bloody hell, haven't heard from you in a while. Don't tell me, you need another bloody favor."

"'Fraid I do. We've got a spike in chatter on our end. We think there's something going on in northern Burma. Maybe a shift in power between the Chinese triads and the Thai syndicates. You got anyone local who might be able to look in on things?"

"Well…" Morris put on his poker voice. "We might have a few lads on the ground. Might cost you a bit of the old share-and-share-alike, then."

"I expect nothing less."

"Give me an hour, and I'll get back to you with a list of likely suspects."

"You're the man, Morris."

"And don't you bloody forget it," agreed the English intelligence officer. "I'll get back to you."

Marchant hung up and considered his options. The Chinese had paid him well, very well, but they were having problems closing the deal; and if they didn't get the notebook and Miss Na, he wasn't going to get the back half of his payment. However, he had an insurance policy in case of just such an event. Marchant decided it was time to cash in, and perhaps add another zero to his offshore bank account in the Cayman Islands. He picked up a third phone and turned on his voice scrambler. A woman's voice answered on the first ring and spoke English with a heavily inflected accent. "Yes, Variance?"

"Is your team ready?"

"They are standing by."

"I am transmitting you real-time information now." Marchant began clicking keys on his computer. "Operation Karttikeya is a go."

"Acknowledged, Variance."

Tom Marchant leaned back in his chair and finished his cognac. Karttikeya was the Hindu god of war.

THEY WEREN'T GOING TO make it. Lily Na had vomited three times, but she half ran half staggered on without complaint. Jungle warfare was not her forte.

Bolan came to an ugly decision. "Nyin. Carry her. Get her to Myitkyina and steal aboard a train or a boat." Bolan pulled a spare pare of batteries for the phone he had given Nyin and pressed them into the his hand. "I'll catch up."

Nyin hefted his carbine. "Let me. I will buy you time."

"I don't speak the lingo. She stands a better chance with you."

Bolan looked up through the trees. They were starting to lose the light. "If you don't hear from me in twenty-four hours, use the phone I gave you and contact British intelligence."

"But—"

Bolan grabbed the front of Nyin's shirt and locked eyes with him. "Get her out of here!"

Nyin stared up into the burning blue eyes of the big American. "Yes, Cooper." He walked up to Lily. "Come. We must go."

Lily's knees were wobbling where she stood and her face was ashen. A breeze would have knocked her over, but there was none to be had in the fetid air beneath the forest canopy. Nonetheless, there was defiance in her exhausted eyes. She shook her head as she struggled to breathe. "No…Cooper. We must—"

"Forgive indignity, Miss Na." Nyin took her by the wrist and put her into a fireman's carry across his shoulders. "We must go."

Lily's eyes were already closed, whether passed out or simply beyond caring was not readily apparent. Nyin adjusted his burden and gave Bolan a nod. "Good luck. Kill many of them."

The little Burmese broke into an encumbered trot and disappeared down the trail.

Bolan turned and loaded a white-phosphorus grenade into his launcher as he moved back the way they had come. He spoke into the mike in his PDA. "Base, this is Striker, how close are they?"

"Five hundred yards back along the trail," Barbara Price replied.

A fallen log supported by a clump of rocks made a good firing position. Bolan dropped to one knee and waited. It was turning dim, but his optic drank up the light beneath the trees. The lead tracker broke into view. The rest of the Chinese team appeared in the distance behind him. Bolan let the tracker move out of sight of the rest of the party behind a stand of trees and fired. The subsonic .308 bullet was slow, heavy and silent, and the tracker's arms flapped as if he'd been hit in the chest with an invisible bowling ball. Bolan worked the bolt of his rifle as the tribesman sidled two steps sideways and collapsed off the trail into the trees.

The Executioner picked up his spent shell and waited.

About half of the Chinese team trotted forward. The remaining Naga pulled up short as he became aware that the bare footprints of his fellow tracker had suddenly come to an end. The tribesman snarled as Chinese infiltration troops took up firing positions. The man poked at the ground with the edge of his ax and began to turn toward where his fellow had fallen.

Bolan shot him between the shoulder blades.

The Naga fell face-first into the muck. Two of U Than's leg breakers stared down at him stupidly. One even kicked the Naga angrily and inquired what his problem was. Then he saw the spreading stain on his tunic. The gangster began waving his arms and screaming. The other gangster slapped him to shut him up. The Chinese hissed and snarled at both of them. Bolan shot Slappy through the head, and Screamy shrieked as he was sprayed with blood and brains.

Screamy went running back down the trail and Bolan let him.

The Chinese stayed focused and swept the landscape with the optical sights of their Chang Feng submachine guns. At a hundred meters, Bolan was at the limit of their effective range. For Bolan and his scout rifle the range was point-blank. One of the weapons tracked his way, and Bolan squeezed his trigger. The Chinese sat down heavily as the bullet burst through his sternum. The remaining two gangsters began spraying blindly into the forest. Bolan dropped another trooper with a bullet to the brain.

Down the trail, Screamy rose into the air. Maung had stepped out of nowhere and seized him by the throat. Maung slammed the Thai to the dirt and roared at him. Bolan raised his crosshairs. Killing Maung would most likely unman the rest of U Than's thugs. Bolan began taking up slack on the trigger. Maung suddenly broke into a run toward the lead team. Bolan shifted his shooting crouch—

Rotten wood exploded in Bolan's face.

The Executioner rolled away, blinking. The Chinese sniper was out there. Bolan heard the boom of the big rifle above the chatter of the submachine guns, but he had no idea where the shot had come from. He was pinned down and already he could hear the shouting as the Chinese team consolidated and coordinated. Bolan's hand trailed across his bandolier and its dwindling supply of grenades. He pulled out a pair of gray canisters the size of beer cans instead. He pulled the pins and tossed the cans over his cover. A spray of automatic weapons fire answered.

Bolan took a bandana out of his pocket and soaked it in water from his canteen as gray smoke poured over the rocks and rose into the trees. Bolan tied the bandana over his mouth and nose like a bandit in an old Western movie and slitted his eyes.

Down the trail, attack whistles shrilled and Chinese came forward. It was clear their quarry had popped smoke to escape the searching scope of the sniper and break contact. The Chinese rushed him before he could disappear into the expanding cloud. Unfortunately for them, their quarry did not try to sneak away. He stayed right where he was. His knife and tomahawk filled his hands as the thud of boots and the slap of sandals approached at full charge.

The Chinese ran straight into the tear gas.

Bolan rose with steel in both hands. He ripped the blade of his knife across the windpipe of a Chinese soldier. The tomahawk rose up in a looping overhand blow and the ax blade crunched through the crown of a Burmese gangster's skull. A Chinese trooper stumbled toward Bolan, but the gas was too thick to tell friend from foe. Bolan had nothing but foes in the burning cloud. The Chinese gasped and folded around Bolan's blade has he took it to the hilt. The man hung on the end of the knife with a belly full of stainless steel. A chop of the tomahawk to the back of his neck ended his suffering.

Bolan could hold his breath longer than many human beings, but there were few more powerful human exertions than combat. Bolan was forced to breathe. He inhaled through his mouth to keep the fiery pain out of the more sensitive linings of his nasal passages as long as possible. He set the pain aside as a hulking figure came through the gas with a blade in hand. The wavy blade of a *kris* dagger filled his hand. The wet crunch of the tomahawk into his temple ended his life.

It was time to go.

Bolan ignored the agony of his burning lungs and broke into a sprint down the trail. He still had kilometers to cover.

CAPTAIN DAI WAS SPEECHLESS.

His remaining two Naga trackers were dead. Two of U Than's muscle-bound Thai bullyboys were dead. Far worse, he had lost five of his own men. Even more appalling was that four of the nine casualties had clearly been killed in hand-to-hand combat.

"Private Su!" Dai snarled.

The sniper presented himself front and center and saluted. "Yes, Captain."

"By my hearing you fired three times."

"Yes, Captain."

Dai stared at the young sniper sourly, already knowing the answer to his next question. "Did you hit anything?"

Private Su shriveled beneath his commanding officer's gaze. "No, Captain."

Su's dressing-down was interrupted as Private Xing ran up to report. "Captain! We have tracked the American past the gas, but the trail disappears."

The American had left the trail and gone into the jungle.

Private Xing finished the thought with a look at the corpses of the last two Naga trackers and shrugged. Xing had no confidence in his skill to track the American through the jungle, and frankly, neither did Dai. The captain silently called on his ancestors for strength. After a moment's thought, he decided he would have to call on someone else for strength. He turned to Private Po.

"Po, get Captain Kyi on the line."

"TRACK 4! TRAIN LEAVING!" Nyin's voice shouted through the speaker in Bolan's PDA. "Train leaving now!"

"I see it!" Bolan rasped and saved the rest of his burning, ragged breath for running. His lungs felt like torn leather bags in his chest. He sprinted through the gloom of the train yard. Many of Burma's trains were still coal-burning steam locomotives that had survived from the days of British colonialism. Bolan saw the train leaving on track 4. The steam whistle gave a final pair of toots, and the locomotive began to grind forward on a long curve toward the mountains. Bolan cut across the train yard to head it off.

Nyin's squat form rose from the roof of a closed boxcar and waved frantically. Bolan redoubled his efforts as the train chugged on, its speed increasing. Nyin dropped to the coupling between the cars and thrust out his hand.

A startled yard bull stepped out of a line shack to find Bolan bearing down on him. His cigarette dangled from his lips in shock. One hand went to the whistle around his neck and the other clawed for the pistol holstered on his hip. Bolan's forearm clotheslined him across the clavicles. The big American stumbled and nearly fell from the impact, but he got his boots beneath himself and charged on. He caught up with the train, but beside him was a flatcar loaded with lumber and the rest of the cars back to the caboose were much the same, flat, high off the ground with little to grab on to.

Bolan put everything he had left into a last forty-yard dash for the boxcar two car lengths down the line. Nyin hung out from the side of the boxcar, extending his arm as Bolan raced the train. The little man's teeth flashed in the dark as he shouted over the clank, chug and hiss of the train. "Nyin see this in movie once!"

Bolan leaped.

His hand slammed around Nyin's wrist, and Nyin's own hand clamped around Bolan's like a vise in the mountain climber's handshake. Bolan's boots went out from underneath him and Nyin groaned as he took the full weight of Bolan and his gear. The Executioner's feet kicked up rocks and chunks of coal as he was dragged along the track. Nyin made a horrible noise and heaved. Bolan swung a foot up and got a boot against the clanking coupling. He narrowly avoided having his toes snipped off by the huge, shifting iron joint and grabbed a cleat on the side of the boxcar. Bolan pulled himself in and clung to the side of the boxcar.

The two men climbed to the top of the boxcar, then flopped down at Lily's feet. Bolan struggled for breath as Lily knelt and opened a canteen. "Why don't the two of you rest? I will take the first watch."

Bolan suspected that was going to be the best offer he was going to get for a while.

8

Vajra 1 screamed across Burma scant yards above the treetops. The black-painted battle helicopter was flying nap of the earth, hugging the jungle canopy and flying around and between hills and mountains rather than over them. The pilot was depending on his skill, his Forward Looking Infrared Radar and, most importantly at the moment, luck. The Mi-25 was the export version of the Russian Mi-24 Hind gunship. It was the largest, fastest, most heavily armed helicopter in the world. The black Hind had been heavily modified with updates to its sensors, imaging, communications and electronic warfare equipment.

Vajra was Sanskrit for Thunderbolt, and Vajra 1 was the pride of the Indian special forces.

However, this was an unauthorized military incursion into an allied nation's airspace. They were almost two hundred miles into northern Burma. There would be no way to explain this away as pilot error or navigational failure. Hinds were not only the most powerful helicopters on Earth, but unlike any other gunship they also had a troop compartment, and the eight-man Indian army jungle-warfare team occupying it would also be equally hard to explain. However, India herself had helped Burma upgrade her air defense grid, and they knew its capabilities well. They were flying beneath Burmese air-defense radars, and the Burmese had nothing in their helicopter fleet that could catch them. Flying nap of the earth and without lights, the Hind was little more than a passing roar in the night heard only by mountain villagers living in huts.

The pilot spoke into the intercom. "Five minutes to LZ, Subedar."

"Thank you, Havildar." Subedar Sikander Singh did not look up from the telemetry he was receiving across his laptop. At six foot six, he was a mountain of bone and muscle, and when he stood, he was shaped like a tombstone wearing a turban. His turban, beard and the wickedly curved *kirpan* dagger he carried on his web belt identified him as an adherent to the Sikh religion. He finally looked up and glanced around at the other seven raid-suited men in the cabin. "Weapons and equipment, final check."

The men checked their gear and shrugged into their packs. Karttikeya Team was packing light. Its members intended to avoid confrontations if possible, but if confrontations were thrust upon them, they intended to finish them. Each man carried a sound-suppressed Tavor assault rifle and a dizzying array of grenades and explosives. The team was made of men from throughout the Indian subcontinent, and their personal collection of sinuously curving steel would give even the local Burmese blade aficionados pause.

Subedar Singh closed his laptop and stood as the red warning light came on in the cabin. "Men, the mission is sudden, danger-ous and politically sensitive. Yet you are the best of the best. You have all been well briefed. The target has been acquired. We have received final confirmation. The mission is go. There are three within the target party. The woman and the laptop she pos-sesses are crucial. Try to take her alive. Intelligence reveals she is with an American, most likely a special operative. They have with them a native guide who is unfortunately an MI-6 drug interdiction asset. On top of that, Chinese infiltration troops appear to be hot on their trail."

Naik Guptas raised his hand. "What are our rules of engage-ment, Subedar?"

"The woman and the information she carries are of the highest national concern. Anyone who stands in the way of their acqui-sition is to be considered a direct threat to India."

The men in the cabin grinned back at their commanding officer. England, the United States, China…in the jungles of Burma it was going to be open season on the superpowers. The pilot's voice spoke over the intercom. "Subedar, we are over the railway. Prepare to deploy."

BOLAN'S EYES FLICKED OPEN. He caught the hard, bright gleam of the naked blade behind him just as it began to plunge toward his chest. With both hands he caught the wrist holding the blade. He lashed his boot up and back to crack the crouching man's jaw. The assassin easily blocked the kick with his forearm and drove his hand down in a hammer blow. Bolan saw stars as Old Man Cao's iron fist collided with his skull.

Lily leaped to her feet and pushed off the safety of her Uzi. Cao's kick slapped the weapon out her hands and sent it spiraling into the night. He spun and kicked again, driving his heel into her belly and dropping her to her knees gagging. Nyin was a motionless lump at the other end of the boxcar's roof. Bolan ignored the pulsing purple lights around the edge of his vision and leaped to his feet. The quarters were too close, and there was no time to grab and shoulder his rifle. His vision swam for a second as his boots hit the roof, but he filled his hands with his knife and tomahawk.

Old Man Cao smiled. The double-edged dagger blade of his knife seemed to drink in the starlight. The PRC was still in the habit of chrome-plating their blades as a cheap way to rustproof them, and it had saved Bolan's life. Cao shook his head at the weapons Bolan brandished. They both knew who was the martial-arts master and who wasn't.

"Give up," Cao said in heavily accented English.

Bolan knew he had only one shot and waited for it. "No."

Cao sighed and pulled a bulky Type 67 silenced pistol from beneath his tunic. "Give up or I shoot both of your knee—"

Bolan hurled his tomahawk. It was a weak throw, a snap of the wrist rather than a wind up and pitch, but the titanium blade was razor keen. Bolan wasn't aiming at Cao's head or chest, but aimed instead for the hand presenting the pistol. Cao's middle, ring and little finger were severed at the second knuckle. The tomahawk clattered to the roof among the scattered digits. The thick black tube of the silencer dipped, and the pistol hung by the trigger guard of Cao's remaining finger for a split second before his hand spasmed and the two-pound pistol dropped.

Bolan cleared the four feet between them in an eye blink.

He slammed his hand against Cao's other wrist and pinned it and the knife he held against his chest. Bolan held his own blade edge up and punched it into the pit of Cao's belly. He ripped the knife upward until the steel met Cao's sternum. Cao sighed and sagged into Bolan's arms with his guts spilling out into the night.

Bolan lowered Cao to the boxcar roof and swiftly patted him down. He commandeered the spare magazine for the silenced pistol. Cao had a cell phone. Bolan committed the last three numbers received to memory, relieved it of its battery pack and hurled it into the night. He took the currency notes in the assassin's sash and then pushed his corpse off the train into the inky darkness below.

Bolan knelt beside Lily. "I need to check on Nyin. You okay?"

The Taiwanese woman gasped. "If I vomit one more time, I believe I will see my shoes."

Bolan nodded. She was still salty. He moved to Nyin. The Burmese man lay in a heap. Blood oozed from his temple, but a quick probe revealed it to be an impact wound rather than a bullet hole. Bolan shook him lightly and he roused with a groan. Words came out in Burmese until his eyes focused and he stared up at Bolan. "They got past me?"

Bolan shrugged. "Yeah."

"I am honorable brother of the Naga, hunted with them, took head with them. I thought no one could sneak up on Nyin. Then you, now Chinese asshole." Nyin shook his head and winced at the pain the effort earned him. "Nyin getting old."

Bolan smiled in the night. Nyin would do. Both his teammates had sand. "You feel sick?"

"No, head feel like broken melon, but no concussion."

Bolan didn't argue. "Sip some water. They know we're on this train, but last check-in the Chinese didn't have any planes over Burmese airspace. If they want us that bad, it will take them at least half an hour to get a strike fighter on top of this train, and my people will warn me before that happens. I want to make as much distance as possible before we hop off."

"Right." Nyin nodded. "See to woman. Nyin will—" he let out a disgusted sigh "—stand guard."

9

The locomotive blew up. Burning chunks of coal streaked upward into the night like meteors. The burning engine continued on down the line while the coal tender derailed and toppled over, spilling several tons of coal beside the track while the two cars behind it crashed and crumpled.

Bolan awoke to find himself flying from one end of the boxcar to the other. He put a hand on the roof and rolled to his feet with inches to spare. The ancient steam train had been wheezing through the mountain passes, and its decrepitude and lack of speed had saved his life. Nyin clung to a cleat, and he held Lily by one arm as she dangled over the side of the car. The water buffalo in the car beneath them bellowed and moaned in consternation.

Nyin glared accusingly as he hauled Lily back up. "Thought you say you know before air strike happen, GI!"

Bolan's rifle had clattered off into the dark with the impact of the crash. The silenced Chinese pistol filled his hand. "That wasn't an air strike. Someone cut the track and uncoupled the engine with an explosive charge." Bolan coughed as a thick cloud of coal dust filled the air from the overturned fuel car. The locomotive continued on whistling and screaming down the line like a flaming banshee. Bolan dropped flat as the crew compartment exploded anew. It wasn't a secondary explosion. Bolan recognized the crack of a hand grenade. The engineer and his crew had almost certainly been killed when the engine blew, but someone had just made sure.

The enemy was undoubtedly all around them.

Bolan coughed again as his battered lungs were assaulted anew. The coal dust filled the air like a black, lung-filling fog.

Bolan eyes slitted as raid-suited figures appeared on either side of the track ahead. They peered into the burning engine car and then began loping down the track toward the remains of the decapitated train. One was clearly consulting some sort of tracking device. Bolan counted four, and more would be waiting in the dark for the big American and his team to fire and make their whereabouts known. Bolan's commandeered assassination pistol was neither particularly powerful nor accurate. He would have to let them get close. There was no doubt he could get one or two, but the rest would put him in a cross fire with their automatic weapons, and if they failed, the men waiting in the dark would pick him off with ease.

The killers trotted toward the fog of coal dust and smoke.

Bolan had an idea. "Nyin, get Lily in the boxcar and hunker down. Leave the door by you open. Cover your ears and eyes."

"But Coop!" Nyin protested. "You—"

"Do it!"

Nyin dropped Lily to the tracks and hopped down beside her. He yanked open the sliding door, and the already agitated water buffalo groaned as the two of them leaped into the car. Their movement didn't go unnoticed. The four killers broke into a run like coursing wolves. Bolan knew there was no way his team could win a firefight, but this night fire was Bolan's friend. A coal-dust explosion was the most feared of all accidents in the coal-mining community. Miners could survive for days after a cave-in, but a fuel-air explosion would rip through the shafts and turn them into kilns of death. All a fuel-air explosion required was fuel, air and a significant source of heat. Bolan had the dust cloud of an overturned coal car and the rarified air of the Burmese night. As for heat…

The soldier drew a white-phosphorus grenade from his web gear and pulled the pin.

The assault team charged through the cloud of dust, and the cotter lever of Bolan's grenade pinged away. He spiraled the grenade straight and true toward the mound of spilled coal. Bolan had exactly three seconds. It took him one to grab the lip of the boxcar and swing himself like a gibbon into the cattle enclosure.

The second was eaten in the time it took him to slam the door closed. In the third, Bolan dropped between two startled beasts and covered his eyes with his palms and thrust his thumbs into his ears.

Armageddon occurred.

Bolan's vision went orange through his pressed fingers and eyelids. The concussion rippled through his flesh like a tsunami. Fire squirted through the ventilation holes and the outrage of the buffalo rose several octaves, but the steel skin of the boxcar deflected most of the blast wave. Bolan rose instantly and was rewarded by being crushed between two of the bucking buffalo. The back of his rib cage and his sternum crackled as they closed in to pinch his heart as he was pinned between four thousand pounds of pot roast. They bucked away in an instant, but Bolan dropped to hands and knees and drew a ragged breath as his ears rang. It hurt like hell but no ribs sawed into his lungs. Something might be cracked or splintered, but nothing was broken and both of his lungs bellowed and cringed as they took in the stench of smoke, dust and fire. "Lily…Nyin…"

Lily rose and fell dizzily against the side of the boxcar. She flinched as the steel singed her. "Nyin is hurt."

Bolan waited as the bucking of the buffalo dropped to shivering and shuddering and made his way through the maze of the enclosures. Nyin had been brained once this night and he undoubtedly had enjoyed every ounce of overpressure the explosion had tried to introduce into the boxcar. "Fatso, we gotta move. Can you walk?"

"Walk the hell out of here…" Nyin rolled to his right and threw up. Bolan was pretty sure if he hadn't had a concussion before he had one now.

"Gotta go, man. Gotta go."

Nyin reeled to his feet and shouldered his Uzi unsteadily. "Right!"

Bolan steadied him and pointed the Burmese in the least likely direction to be kicked to death by a water buffalo. "Lily?"

The spy's nose was bleeding, but whether that was concussion damage or collateral damage from collision with a buffalo

Bolan didn't have time to determine. She gave him a shaky smile and brandished her Uzi. "I am ready."

Bolan yanked his sleeve down over his hand for insulation and pulled the door back. It slid three feet in its twisted track and stuck. He jumped down with his pistol ready. White smoke from the white-phosphorus marking grenade filled the air in dense clouds. It mixed with the black smoke from the coal-dust explosion to obscure nearly everything. White phosphorus burned with terrible heat, and the remains of the unblasted coal had ignited like a barbecue. The pile glowed and burned like Vulcan's forge.

Bolan covered his mouth and nose and squinted against the burning stench, smoke and heat. They had a few precious moments to move while the remaining enemy couldn't see them. "Go! Go! Go!"

Nyin and Lily piled out.

Bolan knelt beside a body.

The smoldering corpse was not in good shape, but a quick inspection told him plenty. Neither the Chinese infiltration troops tracking them nor the Burmese army carried sound-suppressed Israeli Tavor assault rifles. Few Burmese were six feet tall, and though the man's face was a burned and blasted mess, even fewer Burmese could grow a full mustache and beard. His turban had been blasted off and most of his hair burned away, but the scorched iron bangle on the dead man's wrist sealed the deal.

He was a Sikh.

India was definitely in play.

Bolan took the man's pistol and spare magazine from its holster and a .25-caliber Walther TPH stainless-steel pocket pistol he found in his ankle holster. Every plastic piece of furniture on the man's rifle was a twisted and melted mess, and Bolan abandoned it. He rose and spied his own rifle lying by the tracks a few feet away. The plastic stock was scorched, but otherwise it seemed serviceable.

Nyin choked and hacked in the smoke. "Which way?"

That was an excellent question. But there was a more immediate one. They were being tracked, and not just by Naga reading trail sign. The Chinese infiltration team had gotten a man on the train. The Indians had cut the track and assaulted. Bolan and his people were being tracked from on high. "Lily, how is your government tracking you?"

The woman's hand instinctively went to the cross around her neck.

Bolan nodded. "Give it to me."

The woman's beautiful eyes narrowed. "I am not an American asset, and without this my government will have no idea where I am."

"The Chinese and Indian special forces seem to know exactly where we are."

Lily's right hand strayed toward the grip of her submachine gun. "One might equally suspect the security breach to have originated with U.S. intelligence." Her eyes flicked to Nyin. "Or British."

Nyin's eyes widened in the mask of blood covering his face. "Screw you, Hot Pants!" He pointed at his battered head. "I do this for you!"

They were running out of time. Bolan nodded. "She's right, Nyin. Fact is, we don't know who's screwing us. So we go dark. All of us. Give me back the phone I gave you."

Nyin handed over the phone.

"And your own."

Nyin scowled but scrounged in his bag and slapped his own personal phone into Bolan's hand. The soldier took the two phones and hurled them into the glowing pile of coal. "Lily."

The Taiwanese agent took the cross from around her neck and hurled it into the forgelike heat. Bolan typed a final message into his PDA.

"Going dark."

He stripped the device off his forearm and hurled it into the coals. His team was smashed up. His own lungs were still seared by the CS gas and choked with dust. "Nyin, we have to get out of here, and we need someplace to lay low. You got any ideas?"

"Myitkyina biggest town in north. Lots of places to hide. Best place to find new ride, but enemy most likely expecting that. Next town down line Hopin. Most likely they waiting for us there, too."

"We need to go off the radar for a while. I'm talking disappeared."

Nyin gazed up at the stars, then at the compass in his watch and did some mental navigation. "Not sure of our exact location. Know better with daylight. But to west is a Buddhist temple. Not on road. Not on river. Middle of nowhere. Might be best bet."

West was the wrong way to the Thai border, but without holing up and recuperating Bolan knew his team wasn't going to get anywhere. "How far?"

"Twenty kilometer? Forty? Not sure, but sure one hell of lot of hills in between."

Bolan nodded. "Then we'd better get started."

SUBEDAR SIKANDER SINGH'S head rang like a temple gong. His eyes still pulsed with colors from the flash of the blast. Even back in the trees, the explosion had knocked him off of his feet. Battle instincts won the hard way throughout the Asian subcontinent took over. His hand sought and found his weapon and he leaped to his feet. His vision swam, and when it cleared, what he saw was little better.

Thick clouds of smoke rose into the sky. The coal car and the four cars behind it were gone. The three wooden boxcars behind the coal car were burning, while the two metal boxcars were smoldering. Black-and-white smoke twisted together in melding clouds like lovers. Through the smoke an orange light glowed like the entrance to hell. "Guptas!" Singh shouted into his radio.

The radio crackled.

"Naik! Report!" Singh snarled.

There was no response from Naik Guptas.

"Bhuvan…Kaur…Goli…Fire Team One, any unit! Report!"

The radio crackled as Lance-Naik Mohammed reported from farther up the hill where he had sat with his sniper rifle. "Subedar. Mohammed reporting. I saw Guptas and Kaur from my position. They were—" his voice broke "—engulfed in the explosion.

Bhuvan and Goli were flanking them on the other side of the train. They…"

Singh's face was set in a stonelike mask. He had lost half his section in an eye blink. "Fire Team Two, all units, report."

Raj and Parvin reported back. Subedar Singh came out of the trees. "Mohammed, hold position. Parvin, Raj, search for survivors."

Parvin and Raj came out of their firing positions. Singh came upon the burned body of Naik Guptas and moments later the scorched corpse of Kaur. Singh said a quick prayer and continued his sweep. The last report from Guptas had been that the enemy had been spotted leaping from the top of the seventh car down the line and then inside. The seventh car was scorched black, and the water buffalo trapped inside shuddered and twitched. There was no sign of the woman or her companions, and it was too dark to track them.

Parvin reported from the other side of the stricken train. "Subedar, we have located Bhuvan and Goli. Neither survived the explosion. What do you wish to do with their bodies?"

Singh couldn't have their bodies rotting with the tropical heat in the helicopter. He glanced back at the heat mirages shifting over the white-hot coal pile. Both Hindus and Sikhs practiced cremation. "Take their tags and then bring their bodies and all identifying equipment and put them into the fire."

"Affirmative, Subedar."

Indian satellite intelligence had chosen a number of secluded landing zones in the sparsely populated highlands where they could set down the Hind and camouflage it with the netting in stores. Singh spoke into his radio. "Vajra 1, this is Singh."

The pilot came back instantly from his position two klicks down the track. "I read you, Subedar."

"We have taken casualties. Targets' whereabouts currently unknown. Prepare for immediate extraction and plot course for Landing Zone C."

"Affirmative, Subedar. ETA one minute."

Singh was down to four men, but he had satellite recon on his side, Indian intelligence was well entrenched in the Union of Burma and he just so happened to have a Hind gunship. The mission was far from over, and wherever the American and his charges were headed, they had a very long walk ahead of them.

10

Bolan staggered to a halt at the foot of the temple steps. The tiny temple clung to the mountainside, and until one got within fifty yards, it was nearly obscured by the towering trees surrounding it. Climbing the almost vertical goat path that led up the mountain had nearly killed Bolan and his team. The midday sun beat on him like a hammer. Lily was a deadweight in his arms. Nyin looked like a dead man walking. He stood swaying on his feet as a gong rang somewhere within the walls. A five-times life-size Buddha sat at the top of the steep, narrow steps in the lotus position and gazed down at them with a benevolent smile. Bolan took it as a good omen.

The red-painted gate opened, and a three-man phalanx of Buddhist monks descended toward them. The men had shaved heads and wore the red-and-saffron robes of the Theravada Buddhist tradition. They had perfect posture and were somewhere between thirty-five and sixty-five years old.

The lead monk peered up at Bolan for long moments. He took in the unconscious woman in Bolan's arms and Nyin, who appeared to be sleeping standing up. "You are an American," the monk proclaimed.

"You speak excellent English," Bolan countered.

"I studied comparative religions at the University of California, Berkeley, 1967." A smile that matched that of the carved Buddha guarding the temple entrance ghosted across the monk's lips in memory. "Summer of Love, baby. Good time to be a foreign exchange student."

"I can imagine." Bolan liked the monk immediately. "My name is Cooper."

The abbot's smile briefly reappeared. "Somehow, I doubt that."

Bolan shrugged.

The abbot sighed. "My name is Ba-Maw. I am the abbot here. The two worthy gentlemen beside me are Thet and Hlang."

The two flanking monks smiled and bowed deeply. Bolan was somewhat burdened at the moment but bowed his head back respectfully. Nyin fell face-first to the dust and lay unmoving.

Bolan sighed. He would have liked nothing better at the moment than to join him. "We need your help."

"I can see that." Ba-Maw took a long hard look at Bolan's raid suit, the scorched rifle over his shoulder and the weapons and gear festooning his frame. "You are a soldier."

Bolan saw no reason to lie and doubted the monk would believe him if he did. "The woman's Taiwanese intelligence. My prostrate friend is a local drug-interdiction asset for MI-6."

"I gather you are on the run?"

"From Chinese and Indian intelligence."

The monk cocked his head. "Not the Burmese government? Or any of the rebel armies?"

"Not yet," Bolan conceded. "But I'm working on it."

"Is it permitted to ask why you are in Burma, and why both India and the People's Republic of China, who were both allies of ours the last time I went into town, would be pursuing you through the mountains, undoubtedly without the knowledge, much less the permission, of my government?"

"We have something they want."

The abbot nodded patiently.

Bolan laid his cards on the table. "Chinese ballistic missile technology."

For a moment Ba-Maw lost his inscrutable-abbot face. He looked Bolan up and down. "You are covered with blood. Literally and figuratively."

Bolan didn't deny it. "Oh, and the drug lord? U Than?"

The monk simply stared. "I have heard of him."

"Well, you should probably know. He's pretty perturbed with us, too."

"You wish me to risk my temple and the lives of my brother monks to give sanctuary to soldiers, spies and the technology of mass destruction."

Bolan nodded. "Yeah."

The abbot raised an eyebrow. "One wonders what the Buddha would say about this."

"I once read that any man can be a Buddha on top of a mountain." Bolan gazed meaningfully around the verdant forest covering the mountainside. "But the real test is to manifest the Buddha nature down in the red dust of the earth."

Ba-Maw regarded Bolan sourly as he was forced to eat his own Buddhist aphorism. "And you, in your generosity, have brought the red dust of the earth up the mountain with you so that my brother monks and I may test our teachings." The abbot paused and looked and Lily. "Women are not permitted within the temple walls."

Bolan regarded the abbot dryly. "I'll just leave her right here, then."

The abbot's shoulders sagged in defeat. "Very well, bring the woman. Thet and Hlang will bring your friend. They do not speak English, and I believe that is in their best interest. I will not tell them of spies and thermonuclear weapons." Ba-Maw ran a resigned eye over Lily's body. "She will be more than enough to test the brothers' resolve."

BOLAN TOOK HIS MEAL with the monks in the courtyard. The monks had drawn him a hot bath, given him some tea and shown him to one of the little huts behind the temple. Bolan had spent the next eighteen hours sleeping. He'd awoken to the gong announcing the midday meal to find his raid suit had been washed and mended. He would have felt any attempt to remove the silenced Chinese pistol in his right hand or the Indian pistol beneath his pillow, but he was pleased to note none of his other weapons or gear had been moved.

Bolan also noted there was a neatly folded monk's robe and some hastily constructed straw sandals next to his own clothing.

Bolan took the hint. He had been in Southeast Asia many times, and he wrapped the scarlet cloth around his waist and over his left shoulder in the proper fashion. Unfortunately, the robe had been tailored for a monk of Burmese stature. Bolan was a six-footer, and the cotton hugged his frame and the hem barely reached his knees. He looked more like a Roman gladiator than a Buddhist renunciate. He'd tucked the tiny TPH pistol into his robe and gone out to break his fast. The monks had giggled at his appearance as he folded his long legs into a half lotus and joined them.

Like many Buddhist sects, the monks there generally ate one meal a day, served in three nested bowls. However, unlike Zen monks who often had severely regimented diets, temple monks in Southeast Asia, particularly those in the sparsely inhabited highlands, existed on charity. The local villages simply donated whatever they could spare to earn merit. The monks accepted and ate anything and everything they received with gratitude. Bolan suspected he was being feasted as a guest, and the monks were taking the opportunity to gorge themselves on treats.

The first and largest bowl contained pumpkin-and-basil soup. In the second was a little mound of vegetables stir-fried in so much hot red pepper oil it seared Bolan's throat almost as badly as the CS gas had. The smallest bowl contained a few strips of sugar-cured, barbecued beef. Few communities in Southeast Asia could afford the luxury of raising cattle for food. When beef was served, it usually meant some farmer's long-serving water buffalo or ox had finally given up the ghost. The average lifespan of a water buffalo was twelve years, eleven of which would have been spent pulling a plow through the paddies or heavily laden carts through the unpaved mountain passes. Turning the labor-toughened sinews of an ancient ox into something edible was an art form in itself.

Hlang, the temple cook, had outdone himself.

They sat family style, cross-legged on mats around a low wooden table. Bolan suspected the nuclear vegetables may have been some kind of trial by fire, but he'd had the advantage of eating humanity's most challenging cuisine on six continents, and the monks grinned and giggled as the giant American in their midst ate everything set before him with gusto. There were six resident monks in the temple, and another half-dozen teen and preteen "temporary" monks who were ordained for a few months or a few years to gain merit for themselves and their parents, as well as receive an education before returning to village life.

Bolan renested his three now empty and gleaming bowls. He turned to Ba-Maw. "Abbot, may I ask about my friends?"

Lily was strictly forbidden from eating or interacting with the monks other than Thet, who had some medical expertise. Nyin had still been unconscious when they had carried him to one of the little huts behind the temple the monks dwelled in.

Ba-Maw set down his chopsticks. "Miss Na is suffering from exhaustion, both nervous and physical. She half awoke writhing and moaning several times. Brother Thet believes this is what you would describe in the West as night terrors. He believes this is something she has suffered from before."

Bolan could only imagine what the enigmatic beauty had suffered in her life and how it might manifest itself in her psyche. The abuse at the hands of U Than and his thugs was probably the least of it. However, total physical exhaustion and the nearly certain prospect of a horrific and imminent death under torture couldn't be helping matters much. "Can you do anything for her?"

"Rest is what she requires more than anything. Brother Thet has given her massage and a philter of rice wine, herbs and opium so that she may sleep long and without dreams." The abbot let out a long sigh. "Mr. Nyin is suffering from one if not multiple concussions, and the march to come here did him no favors. I have the younger monks watching him constantly, but if there is bleeding within the brain, only surgery will save him, and I must tell you he will certainly die long before we can get him to a hospital. He will live, or he will not. And for you—" Abbot Ba-Maw looked at Bolan pointedly "—rest will be the best medicine."

Bolan knew rest was a luxury he couldn't afford. "You've been very kind, Abbot—"

"Call me Ba-Maw," the abbot interrupted. "My friends do."

"Ba-Maw." Bolan bowed his head in respect. "You have—"

"I have decided to do everything there is in my power so that you and your companions may live. I have not always been a renunciate. I have lived in the world, and I have absolute faith in the suffering my government, the drug dealers they are in league with, as well as the governments of India and China, will inflict upon you should you be captured. I am a Buddhist. You have by your own admission brought the red dust of the earth to the mountain and forcibly reminded me that I am devoted to the end of suffering. The Chinese dragon rises once more, reincarnating itself, hoping once again, as in ages past, to be the greatest superpower. The dragon's current predations, military, political and economic throughout Asia are well-known. The Buddha would say I should look to my own salvation, and whether it is to be found upon this mountain or as my mortal flesh is engulfed in nuclear fire is irrelevant." The abbot's face took on a terrible resolve. "But Ba-Maw the man would have the blade of China's sword known to all, and blunted if possible, and perhaps the balance of power maintained."

"You're putting yourself and your temple in terrible danger."

"No, it is you who has put us in terrible danger when you arrived on our steps. Nevertheless, I have consulted with the brethren and we have chosen to accept that risk."

"I thought you said you weren't going to tell them—"

"Don't contradict me in front of the brothers." Ba-Maw gave Bolan the eyebrow. "They do not speak English, but they are not fools."

"All the more reason for my friends and I to leave immediately."

"You and your companions will leave when you are fit to do so."

"I appreciate your hospitality, but we're a danger to you and your temple. Our enemies would have no compunction about torturing you, killing you and burning this place to the ground. I must leave as soon as my friends are awake and can walk."

The abbot gave Bolan a hard smile. "You may leave whenever you wish, but I'm ashamed to say I have had several of the brothers go to your huts. We have confiscated your weapons and hidden them."

Bolan had suspected that might happen, but he hadn't been willing to booby-trap his equipment to prevent it. "I wish you hadn't done that."

The abbot arched a pragmatic eyebrow. "You still have the pistol concealed beneath your robes. You may shoot us if you wish, but we will not reveal the location of your equipment until you are well enough to make your way."

Bolan was a master of weapons concealment, but the powers of perception of a man who had been meditating for eight hours a day since 1967 were of a higher order and not to be discounted. He admitted defeat and, more than that, he admitted to himself the need for three more meals like this one, and he and his team needed at least another forty-eight hours of rest before they resumed trying to pull themselves out of Burma by their bootstraps.

Bolan pressed his palms together in a prayer position and nodded. "Then I humbly accept your hospitality."

11

"Captain Dai!" Burmese Light Infantry Captain Ohnmar Phyu grinned happily at his Chinese counterpart. Captain Phyu was a head taller than Dai and wore his hair in a military brush cut. Unlike many Asians, he walked with a bantam-rooster strut. The Burmese military might be technologically primitive, but the army had been fighting rebel, revolutionary and separatist guerrilla armies on a dozen fronts for more than half a century. Until very recently, their armor, aircraft and artillery had been antiquated at best and obsolete and down for lack of spare parts at worst. Military intelligence consisted of soldiers running barefoot along mountain game trails. Rather than fast-roping Rangers deploying out of choppers with gunship support, the light infantry hoofed it to the huts of their enemies, and the raids consisted of knives drawn in the dark.

The terrain they fought in rivaled the African Congo for heat, disease and misery, and unlike the Congo, much of it was nearly vertical rather than flat jungle plains. Captain Ohnmar Phyu's nickname was "The Hammer of the North." His men were all veterans and supplied with the best the army had to offer. His men were all armed with locally made copies of the Israeli Galil assault rifle. Phyu had his own personal Praetorian Guard, and the members of this elite hard-core cadre were equipped with body armor, night-vision gear and personal communication equipment.

Dai considered himself the equal of almost any operator on Earth, but even he had to admit he wouldn't want to meet Phyu cutlery to cutlery in some highland culvert by starlight.

Phyu bowed low and clasped his fists. Dai spoke excellent Burmese, but Phyu had no Mandarin or Cantonese so he spoke in English as a neutral language out of respect. "I am honored." He gestured at a wadded tent of camouflage netting. "Will you take tea?"

"I would prefer a lager." Dai knew from long experience that off duty Phyu was a confirmed beer hound.

Phyu led him to the tent and reached into an ancient foam cooler for a pair of Mandalay Red Lagers. He cracked off the caps with his callused hands. He had known Dai for nearly a decade. He knew full well that the captain was an infiltration trooper, but by the same token the PRC often gave the Burmese army intelligence on many of the rebel armies and their movements. Phyu clinked beers with Dai and got right to business. "Would you know anything about the destruction of the eight-o'clock train out of Myitkyina last night?"

Most negotiations in Asia were long and circular affairs. However, time was of the essence, and Dai matched Phyu's directness. "I know much about it."

It was an unexpected tactic, and Phyu considered his beer for long moments. "Tell me you were not involved, my friend."

Dai picked up on the implied threat. "Of course not. The People's Republic of China is a firm ally and trading partner of the Myanmar Union."

"Indeed," Phyu agreed. "However, our friendship did not prevent you from shooting down an airliner in our airspace."

"Most regrettable," Dai conceded. "However, it was a Chinese fighter that shot down a Chinese airliner. My government has and will continue to express its deepest regrets over the incident and its willingness to make amends."

Phyu understood his personal opportunity to profit from the statement well. "I see."

"You must understand, my friend," Dai continued, "the plane simply could not be allowed to reach India, and the Indian government was not pleased, and they have taken action."

Captain Phyu bolted upright. "The Indian government blew up the train?"

"They have inserted a jungle-warfare team. They have a

special-operations Hind gunship hiding somewhere in the jungle, very likely somewhere nearby."

Phyu nearly choked on his beer.

Dai knew he had Phyu's full attention. "You and I are friends. We have exchanged valuable intelligence in the past and trained together. So I will speak plain. Something has been stolen from my government. We wish it back. It is contained in a laptop. I am not prepared to tell you what it is, and I tell you now, without malice or insult, that the information is encrypted and your security services simply do not have the technology to break the code. This is why I sought you out. I believe your discretion can be trusted. I believe it would be best if you and I handled this personally, and it would please me well if my government's gratitude was showered personally upon an old comrade and friend."

Phyu put his poker face back on. "Who has stolen your property?"

"There are three of them, a Taiwanese woman, a local in league with MI-6 and an American commando of some kind. They were on the train when the Indians attacked it. We believe they have escaped and are on foot."

Phyu immediately pulled out a map and spread it across his table. "That was twenty-four hours ago."

"Indeed," Dai agreed.

Phyu began running some calculations using his own men's considerable marching ability as a measuring stick. "Burdened with the woman and given the terrain, I would give them no more than twenty to forty kilometers maximum march." He stabbed a compass needle into the spot along the railway that already had an "X" marked on it where the train had been derailed. He spun the compass around and drew a circle. "I will have men immediately begin circulating their descriptions among the villages within eighty kilometers of the train derailment. I will also post a hefty reward for information." Phyu glanced up. "I trust your government is willing to provide an inducement that the American will not be able to match?"

"I am sure the American is carrying funds with which to help buy his way out of the country and is prepared to extend extravagant IOUs on his government's good credit, but when it comes to peasants, squads of soldiers have the moral advantage over three refugees hiding in the trees." Dai reached into his pocket and produced a newly minted Golden Panda coin. "And gold in the hand gleams far brighter than the promissory notes of a nation half a world away."

BOLAN WATCHED Lily exercise. It was quite something to see, like an erotic fusion of Tai Chi, power yoga and exotic dancing all rolled into one. Lily's body finally came to a halt. Bolan was tempted to applaud, but he remained silent as she stood stone still for long moments with her eyes closed and breathed. She turned her head and raised a bemused eyebrow at Bolan. "Did you enjoy the show?"

"I've seen Chi Kung performed by masters." Bolan shook his head in admiration. "But that was a new one on me."

"It is named the Jade Princess Seduces the Heavens, and is what we call an inner chamber art. It was designed to open the energy pathways of the body and build what we call *jing,* or essence. Less esoterically, it is designed to give a woman a supple, blooming figure, a radiant complexion, as well as complete control over every muscle in her body, both internal and external."

Bolan's mind blurred at the thought, but he kept his expression neutral. "Oh?"

She slowly smiled and the smoldering erotic fire behind her eyes cooled. Bolan felt an aching pang at the loss but grinned anyway.

Her mouth quirked into a rueful smirk. "Seducing you is going to be harder than I thought."

"Bring me beer. Do my laundry." Bolan shrugged. "I'm easy."

"You are a pig."

Bolan was pleased to see that whatever night terrors had tormented her seemed to have passed for the moment. Her feet were another matter. They looked much better, but they would have to march soon and march hard. Bolan held up Nyin's little brown jug of medicated wine. "Foot rub?"

Lily reclined against a pillar. "Always."

Bolan pulled the bottle back slightly. "I thought you said I was a pig."

"You are a charming pig." Lily gracefully kicked off her sandal and extended one perfectly arched foot. Bolan began rubbing the herbed alcohol into her plantar fascia. Lily sighed.

Bolan arched an eyebrow of his own. "Good as Nyin?"

"You have not been trained in the acupressure points as he has." She sagged against the pillar as he firmly slid his thumb along the ball of her foot into the metatarsal arch. "But it is quite clear you have given a woman a foot rub before."

"I saw you looking in on Nyin. How's he doing?"

Lily let out a soft sigh. "He needs more rest, but he will live, and I believe we both know he will walk until he dies if required."

"So will you. I've seen it." Bolan switched feet. "We're going to have to move soon."

"I will be ready."

The temple gong rang in alarm as if on cue. Bolan could hear a pair of sandals slapping up the steep stairway in a sprint. Abbot Ba-Maw and the acolytes spilled out of the meditation hall. The gate opened, and a gasping young monk staggered into the courtyard. He pointed back down the mountain and spoke in breathless, rapid-fire Burmese. Bolan didn't need a translation.

There were soldiers on the mountain.

Abbot Ba-Maw listened to the report and then turned to Bolan with a grim look on his face. "Soldiers are sweeping the villages. Your description and those of your friends are being circulated. Gold is being offered."

"What kind of soldiers?"

"Burmese light infantry."

"Will they come here?" Bolan asked.

Ba-Maw shook his head unhappily. "I do not know. We do not have much in the way of rebels or separatists in this area. The temple has never been searched before." He looked at Bolan holding Lily's foot. "But then again we live in extraordinary times."

"We have to get out of here."

Ba-Maw nodded toward their visitor. "According to young

Shway, this area is swarming with soldiers. The mountain is surrounded below. You would have to sneak through their patrols. I do not like your chances."

Bolan didn't like their chances, either. "You got any place around here to hide?"

"There are some caves near the top of the mountain. Monks from this temple sometimes go up to them to meditate in solitude. However, the paths leading to them are far from hidden."

"Nyin could pass himself off as one of your monks."

"He could. He does have some most extraordinary bruises, but I believe we could be creative enough to hide them. The temples of Southeast Asia are positively infested with little bald men in robes. To soldiers, I am sure we all look the same." Ba-Maw let out a long breath. "You, on the other hand, and the woman…"

Bolan turned to Lily. "I have an idea, but you are going to have to be brave."

12

"Please, Miss Na, do not cry," Nyin pleaded.

Lily Na wept as if it were the end of the world. Bolan held her hand as the razor slid across her skull. There were salons in Los Angeles that would have paid thousands for the silky, blue-black lengths of hair piled around her feet. Thet was the temple barber, as well as medic. He murmured soothing noises as he finished the last few strokes of the razor. Lily's lower lip trembled as he bowed and stepped away. "Is it done?"

Bolan nodded. "It's done."

"I need a mirror."

Abbot Ba-Maw sighed unhappily. He was a Buddhist monk, forsworn of ego, want and desire, but even he was having problems with seeing so beautiful a woman so utterly devastated. "This is a temple. We do not have mirrors."

"Your signal mirror." Lily looked beseechingly at Bolan. "Give it to me."

Bolan had foreseen that request. He was wearing his raid suit once more, and while most of his weapons had been removed they had left him the mirror to shave with along with a few other personal items. Bolan pulled his signal mirror from his thigh pocket and handed it over.

The woman's face went white as she looked at herself in the small sheet of stainless steel. "I look like a victim of cancer."

The shape of her head was exquisite, though they would definitely have to do something about the deathly pallor of her newly shorn skull. They would have to do something about her complexion, as well. It was flawless and stuck out among the brassy skinned Burmese monks. Lily handed back the mirror and sagged into Bolan's arms in a fresh bout of weeping. The Chinese had a saying that a woman's hair was her wealth, and Lily Na was now utterly destitute.

Nyin conferred with the Hlang for a few moments, then turned to Bolan. "Hlang and I will make paste of betel and palm oil to stain skin. Robes will hide feminine figure. She keep her head down? She may pass."

Lily was a trained intelligence agent. Once she got over the moral devastation of being bald, he was sure she could make the act stick. "Good enough."

Nyin peered up at Bolan critically. "What about you, GI Joe?"

That was the million-dollar question. Bolan was tempted to make a solo run down the mountain and go escape-and-evade. There was a good chance that acting alone he could break through the Burmese cordon and they could either link up later or Lily and Nyin could make a break in the other direction while the Burmese soldiers chased him. But Bolan wasn't in the habit of leaving anyone behind. "I'm just going to have to lurk."

TOM MARCHANT SMILED at his screen. He had spoken with Indian and Chinese intelligence agents. Captain Dai, however, was being somewhat reticent. At first Marchant had chalked that up to pride and pouting, but he should have come back clamoring for assistance from on high long before now. Marchant watched the Burmese light infantry move through the mountains of northern Burma through high-resolution satellite imaging. He needed no software to tell him that the sweeps were radiating outward in all directions from the site of the Indian attack on the train. He had it on very good authority that the sweeps were being led by the infamous Ohnmar Phyu, the Hammer of the North, and being spearheaded by *Nagar,* which were Phyu's private squad of veteran raiders. Marchant also had it on very good authority that Captains Dai and Phyu had been in contact on numerous occasions in the past. It was quite clear to him that Dai was running an operation of his own.

Marchant would be good and goddamned before he let Dai's and Phyu's little captains' club edge him out of the bounty on Miss Na and her laptop.

He was running search parameters of his own.

The underworld of every town and city, as well as the police, had been well bribed to be on the lookout for the Na, Nyin and the American. For that matter, there were enough *kyat* notes and gold pieces floating through the villages that the unlikely trio would find no sanctuary. Marchant doubted that the American would be camping out in the wild. They would have very little in the way of survival gear, and by his count they had been in at least three firefights. They would be exhausted, and one or more of them would almost certainly have sustained injuries.

Marchant sat up. He looked at the soldiers sweeping the villages on his screen and knew he'd hit it. There would be no sanctuary in the villages.

Sanctuary was the word.

Buddhist temples had acted as sanctuaries for thousands of years. Marchant began typing new search parameters into his computer that in turn began guiding the lenses of a satellite that gazed down at Burma from space. His computer began printing dots across the map. One dot was on top of a little mountain not far from Lake Indawgyi. The location was perhaps fifteen miles from the train attack and in some very rough country. Infantry units were sweeping the base of the mountain and the villages near the lake but appeared not to have ascended yet. They were undoubtedly cordoning off the mountain before sweeping upward.

Marchant smiled as he calculated the possibilities, and he liked the odds very much. He decided it was time to make two phone calls. The first would earn him his next cash installment from the Indians, and the second would put that little bastard Dai back in his pocket. He would let Subedar Singh in on his suspicions about a little temple on a mountaintop near Lake Indawgyi. Then he would drop a coin on that little prick Dai and let him know that there was a rogue helicopter gunship trying to steal the ball.

That would reset the chessboard nicely.

NAGAR COMPANY STALKED the temple grounds, accompanied by the giant Maung, who was apparently looking after U Than's interests. The monks knelt in the courtyard. Nyin and Na knelt with them. A pair of soldiers stood behind the line of monks with bayonets fixed. Abbot Ba-Maw stood off to one side quietly conferring with the sergeant in charge.

Nyin looked more like a monk than most of the monks did. He and Hlang had done a remarkable job on Lily. Her flawless skin was now the deep copper color of someone who had spent years under the Southeast Asian sun. She was an indescribably beautiful woman, but no one other than Bolan would ever have thought of shaving her head and hiding her in plain sight. Her green eyes would be a dead giveaway, so she kept her eyes closed and her head bowed. She methodically worked the golf-ball-size wooden beads of her monk's prayer necklace as if she were patiently trying to meditate the soldiers away.

So far it was working. The monks knelt with only the abbot receiving any attention.

A squad of heavily armed infantrymen searched the grounds. Bolan had no room to run so rather than escape-and-evade he was forced to play hide-and-seek. He had stood beside the temple gate and, when it had opened to admit the soldiers, he had hidden behind it. Rather than going to ground and waiting to be flushed out he had shadowed his searchers, moving from pillar to pillar as they crossed the courtyard and rousted the monks out of the meditation hall. He'd stayed one doorstep behind them as they shoved their bayonets through the large baskets of rice in the kitchen, and like the tail of a serpent he had shadowed them as they rummaged through the huts in back of the temple. He followed them up the trail to the mountain caves near the summit and let them pass him on the way back down to rejoin them once more like an invisible caboose.

It was a simple but exceedingly dangerous tactic. The one thing in Bolan's favor was that searching men hardly ever looked behind them. Plus Bolan could teach even a ninja a thing or two about hiding. He stayed within spitting distance in the places they had just covered and after two hours found himself back at the temple.

He followed them through the little back gate into the meditation hall and stopped there to watch what was going on in the courtyard. So far it all seemed copasetic. There was no rebel activity in this area. Nagar Company was very unlikely to slaughter monks and burn temples on their home turf without a reason. The sergeant and the abbot seemed to be speaking to each other in a fairly civil manner.

Bolan's eyes narrowed as a pair of soldiers broke away from the group and began walking toward the meditation hall. The sergeant had given no discernible order and the men did not seem to be in any rush. Bolan faded back and moved into the main temple. A golden, gleaming statue of the Buddha sat cross-legged in front of a devotional altar.

The giant Maung knelt before him.

Maung was busily peeling the gold-leaf appliqué from the Buddha's big toe with a Chinese combat knife. The scar tissue that served him for eyebrows rose in alarm as he spotted Bolan and then his eyes narrowed predatorily as he rose. His gaze slid up and down Bolan's frame as if he were reading the American's aura. He smiled to reveal a mouthful of gold-and-silver teeth and spoke in broken English. "No gun?"

Bolan shrugged. "The monks. They hid them."

Maung smiled wider.

The giant had Bolan dead to rights, and they both knew it. One shout from the Burmese boxer and the game was up. For that matter there was twenty feet separating them, and Maung had a knife in hand and a shiny new Chang Feng submachine gun slung over his shoulder.

Bolan had to keep the big man talking.

He looked at the square of bloodstained bandage taped across the boxer's flattened face. "How's your nose?"

Maung scowled and his hand went to his automatic weapon.

Bolan held up his empty hands and waggled his eyebrows and fingers insultingly. "Bet you a *kyat* I can do it again."

Maung's smile stayed painted on his face, but his eyes went cold.

Bolan's knuckles popped and creaked as he balled his hands into fists and then dropped them down to his sides loose and twitching like an Old West gunfighter ready to draw. "Bring it."

Au Maung had risen to the top of Burmese Bando boxing. He had competed against the Thai kickboxers who were the undisputed bad boys of Southeast Asia and beaten them. It was rumored he had participated in illegal matches where men wrapped ropes around their fists, dipped them in paste and rolled them in broken glass. It was said he had won death matches where men wore blades strapped to their feet. The round-eye standing before him had beaten him once and, to his mind, had cheated to do it. The mighty Maung wasn't about to back down from a white man, particularly when he held all the cards. That didn't mean the killer was going to play fair. His knife stayed in his hand.

"Bleed you, white boy," Maung said.

Bolan's signal mirror slid out of his sleeve and undetected into his palm. He had spent half an hour earlier in the morning with some palm oil and a stone sharpening all four edges of the three-by-four-inch scrap of stainless steel and another thirty minutes determining its flight characteristics. It had a pronounced tendency to yaw, but in the end Bolan found if he used a lot of sidearm he could reliably sink it into a pumpkin at ten feet.

He needed to bring Maung in a little closer.

Bolan spit on the ground between them and lifted his chin in a challenge as old as time. The mighty Maung came on with his knife held low. At ten feet Bolan threw. It was a curve ball that would have given a major league baseball pitcher a run for his money. The signal mirror corkscrewed through the air, crazily flashing the reflected the light of the banked temple candles. Bolan had been aiming for Maung's eyes, but he was a little low. The leaf of stainless steel sliced through the bandage covering Maung's face and sank through the remains of his shattered septum. Maung's howl was smothered as fresh blood flooded his sinuses and the back of his throat.

His hands went to his face and Bolan closed.

Maung wore his massive physique like armor plate. Given his expertise in the most brutal forms of kickboxing, his body would be able to withstand incredible punishment, but Bolan well knew that all armor had its weak points. Chinese martial artists called a certain part of the human male anatomy the Golden Target and said, "No man can put his chi there."

Maung keened like an insect as Bolan's boot slammed up under his sarong. He fell to his knees gagging and clutching his crotch. Maung had a neck like a bull, but there were no muscles covering the front of the throat. Bolan looped a punch like a softball pitch under Maung's jaw, and cartilage crunched beneath his knuckles. Maung fell writhing to the floor, blowing red bubbles and drowning in the blood and broken gristle clogging his throat.

Bolan took up Maung's Chang Feng submachine gun, Hi-Power pistol and blade. It was good to have real steel in his hands again, but the problem remained. He had silenced Maung, but sooner rather than later the sergeant would be waiting for Maung to return from his temple looting. Bolan could almost feel the Buddha's eyes following him in quiet disapproval as he dragged Maung's corpse behind the altar. He would have to deal with his karma later. Right now he had a squad of light infantry to deal with. Bolan threaded the sound suppressor over the muzzle of his new weapon and peered out into the courtyard through a crack in the shutter.

All seemed well. There was no sign of alarm. The soldiers had slung their rifles and were now smoking cigarettes and standing around waiting for orders to move out. The sergeant was accepting a small roll of *kyat* notes from the abbot. The sergeant had found nothing untoward in the temple, but he was not above accepting a small bribe to go away. Bolan didn't know where the other two men had gone off to, but if his luck held for just a few more minutes…

There was a shout and commotion from the area of the temple commode, and one of the missing soldiers came running into the courtyard. He was brandishing Bolan's battered scout rifle overhead like a winning lottery ticket. The sergeant whirled on the abbot with a snarl. He pointed back to his radioman while he grabbed the front of Ba-Maw's robe and shouted orders. His pistol came out of its holster, and he cocked back the hammer with his thumb.

Nyin popped up like a jack-in-the-box from where he knelt and slammed a sandaled foot between the sergeant's shoulder blades. The sergeant's pistol discharged into the eaves as he was propelled into a violent embrace with the abbot, and the two men went down in a tangle of limbs. The radioman stared for a fatal second in shock with his handset forgotten. Lily rose and looped the prayer beads she had been wearing around the radioman's throat. The soldier bent back like a bow as Lily heaved on the beads to cinch off his throat and rammed her knee into the small of his back. The soldiers standing around leaped into action and began unslinging their weapons with the practiced speed of veterans.

Bolan slid the barrel of his subgun through the shutter and began firing. One of the guards standing behind the kneeling monks raised his rifle only to drop it again as Bolan printed a pattern of holes in the back of his head. The second guard whirled to take a matching pattern through his face. Bolan shouted to Nyin over the bedlam. "Tell the monks to stay down!"

Nyin shot a soldier with the sergeant's pistol and roared in Burmese. The monks instantly prostrated themselves. Lily came up with the radioman's pistol and shot another. The side door of the temple flew open, and the other soldier who had found Bolan's hidden weapons came flying through with his weapon spraying on full-auto. The wooden shutter Bolan had been firing through exploded in splinters. The shooter was reduced to bloody rags as Bolan held his trigger down and burned his remaining forty rounds into him. He ran to the dead man and relieved him of his rifle and spare magazines and checked the load in the grenade launcher.

The shooting outside had stopped and a shouting match had begun. Bolan stayed low and peered through the crack of the temple's double doors. Nyin and Lily had taken cover on one side of the courtyard behind a pair of stone pillars. The sergeant had lost about half of his squad, but five of them had taken similar cover on the opposite side of the courtyard. Bolan had the grenadier's weapon but outside it was still five against two and Nyin and Lily only had pistols. The sergeant himself held his bayonet across the abbot's throat. The sergeant shouted toward the temple. "Maung!" His voice rose an octave. "Zaw!"

Maung and Zaw were dead.

Nyin shouted, "Coop!" and his own voice grew anxious. "Coop!"

Bolan said nothing. He didn't have a good shot on the sergeant where he stood near the gate, and he wasn't willing to shoot through the abbot. Bolan pulled a fade out the back and ran around the outside of the temple. The shouting match resumed and Bolan knew he had only seconds to act. The sergeant was clearly threatening to kill the abbot if Nyin and Lily didn't surrender, and Bolan was pretty sure in a moment he would do it. The good news was the gate was still open. Bolan stepped through and the sergeant went rigid as the Executioner pressed the muzzle of his rifle against the back of his head. The courtyard suddenly became very quiet. Bolan spoke softly. "Nyin, tell the sergeant to drop the knife."

Nyin tendered the suggestion to the sergeant in Burmese. The sergeant's shoulders tensed, and Bolan gave his weapon a meaningful little push against the sergeant's skull. The knife fell with a ringing noise to cobblestones. Bolan kept his tone calming and quiet. "Abbot, step away."

Ba-Maw stepped to one side and dabbed at the dribble of blood where the point of the bayonet had parted his skin. Bolan eased his weapon off the sergeant's head just slightly. "Tell him to order his men to drop their weapons."

Nyin and the sergeant had a short conversation. Nyin shook his head. "Sergeant say you will kill him and his men."

"Tell the sergeant I have no quarrel with him, his soldiers or his government. Tell him this matter is between me and the Chinese. Tell I am prepared to give him and his men one million *kyat* right now to let us walk away."

At the moment a million *kyat* would trade for about $150,000 American. Bolan could hear the wheels turning in the sergeant's head. Another exchange in Burmese occurred and Nyin sighed. "Sergeant say he has lost men, be in big trouble."

"Tell him to say we ambushed them. There was a firefight. We escaped. One million *kyat* right now, and if I get out of Burma alive my government will compensate him far more. Enough so that he'll never care if he ever makes lieutenant." Bolan ground the muzzle of the Galil into the base of the sergeant's skull as if he were turning a screw. "Tell him he has three seconds to decide. Then I empty the entire magazine of this rifle into his head and discharge the grenade launcher into his men."

Nyin translated. The sergeant shouted the order. His men looked about at one another. The sergeant's voice cracked as he reiterated his order. The five soldiers reluctantly dropped their weapons and shot wary looks around the courtyard.

Bolan removed the muzzle of the rifle but kept the weapon trained on the sergeant. "Tell him to turn around."

The sergeant turned and put up his hands at Nyin's order. Bolan kept his eyes on the man. "Lily."

"Yes, Coop."

"Go to the meditation hall. That's where the monks hid my gear. You'll find a money belt. Bring it. Then gather their weapons."

The sergeant's jaw dropped as he heard Lily speak English and he saw through the ruse. There was nothing to be done about that. The sergeant had shown a determined streak of self-preservation, and Bolan would just have to hope it was matched by his greed. Between the two he might just be able to use the man to get off the mountain. All he needed was his luck to hold a little while longer.

The black Hind gunship rose over the temple walls in a maelstrom of rotor wash and hung in the sky as menacing as the thunderbolt of divine fury it was named for.

13

A voice thundered from the Hind's public address system like God on high. "Lay down your arms! Surrender the woman and the information!"

The command was repeated in Chinese and Burmese. The twin-barrel 30 mm rotary cannon on the chopper's starboard cheek covered the courtyard with its baleful twin stare. The command came across the speaker again in all three languages.

Bolan shouted over the sound of the rotors. "Nyin, stay under the eaves. Lily, stay in the meditation hall. Abbot, get your monks ready to run."

The command blared from above once more and suddenly stopped in midsentence. Bolan figured the pilot had probably noticed by now that the monks were all lying flat and the soldiers didn't have any guns and had reported this strange turn of events to whoever was working the communications suite in the troop compartment. Fast ropes dropped from either side of the troop compartment and slapped down on the stones of the courtyard. Two men began sliding down the fifty feet.

Bolan stepped out from under the eaves and fired his grenade launcher.

He ignored the men roping down and looped his grenade into the Hind's open cabin door. Yellow fire pulsed from the troop compartment and windows blew out on either side. The Hind's tandem cockpits and cabin were separated by armor, but the helicopter lurched from the hit. The fast rope swung as the chopper yawed and one man lost his grip. He plunged forty feet, and his head burst like a water balloon as he hit the cobblestones face-first. The second roper was a big man in a turban, and he managed the remarkable feat of continuing his descent with just one hand and his crossed boots as he ripped off a burst from his rifle that nearly sliced off Bolan's toes. The big American jumped back under the eaves, and the helicopter swung about so the roper would land outside the temple.

"Ba-Maw, get the monks out of here!" Bolan roared. "Nyin, tell the sergeant to get his men out. Go! Go! Go!"

Nyin shouted. The sergeant shouted. Monks and Burmese soldiers began scattering in all directions. Nyin stepped out and began firing his pistol as fast as he could pull the trigger, but the Hind was armored to take hits from 23 mm cannons and his shots did nothing save strike sparks off the windscreen. The helicopter suddenly lunged upward and dipped its nose. The fast roper had landed and it was payback time. Several soldiers spent fatal seconds scooping up their rifles.

The twin-barrelled 30 mm high-velocity automatic cannon erupted into life at thirty rounds per second. The courtyard cratered like the moon beneath the high-explosive shells, and human bodies came apart like piñatas. Chunks and chips of stone flew like shrapnel.

Lily and Nyin cringed under the eaves in precarious, momentary safety. Bolan hurled himself out the temple gate. He rolled to his feet and grimaced as he scanned the grenades in his captured gear. The Burmese soldiers fought against guerrillas and separatist tribesman. None of their enemies had armored vehicles, and there was nothing in the bandolier that could crack Russia's "flying tank."

But he might be able to distract it.

Bolan loaded an M-781 marking round into the grenade launcher's smoking breech. Two soldiers crouched behind pillars in front of the main temple and fired their rifles in long bursts. The Hind pointed its cannon accusingly, and the men, the pillars and the temple flew apart under the onslaught. Bolan unloaded a magazine into the pilot's cockpit window to attract his attention. The Hind turned on its axis and dipped its nose to blast

Bolan apart. The Hind had two tandem cockpits, one for the weapons operator in front and one for the pilot in back. Bolan fired at the pilot and leaped back inside the temple as hell erupted where he had just stood.

Orange smoke exploded around the pilot and was almost instantly whipped away by the rotor wash. The orange dye smearing the armor glass like a giant paintball round was a little more permanent. Bolan slapped a fresh magazine into his rifle and loaded the remaining marking round. The M-781 was used in grenadier training to let soldiers see where their shots were landing. They also had a secondary role in marking targets for air support.

Bolan stepped out and fired.

The Hind came thundering in, and it was clear the pilot could still see well enough to aim his nose at the temple. Bolan's shot hit low and the forward weapons operator cockpit was smeared in a brilliant, lemony sunshine yellow. The paint had no effect on the weapons operator's trigger finger, and the twin barrel cannons pulsed fire. The rounds flew through the open gate and hammered the already collapsing temple hall. The Hind thundered past as it finished its gun run and rose up out of grenade range.

Lily clutched a fallen rifle and stared at Bolan incredulously from cover. "You're shooting it with paint?"

Bolan nodded as he loaded a frag. He'd failed to blind the gunner or the pilot, but with luck it might be enough to keep the chopper from tracking them in the air. They also had to worry about firing half-blindly and obliterating what they'd come to collect. The Hind hung in the air over the mountain as if the pilot and gunner were considering the same thing. Bolan glanced out the gate. The monks had fled outside and miraculously none seemed to have been killed. They wept and shook and stared up fearfully at the dragon hovering high above. "Abbot!"

Ba-Maw stood in plain sight staring at the smoking ruins of his temple. He walked through the gate in a daze and took in the carnage in the courtyard. Bolan put a hand on his shoulder. "I'm sorry."

The abbot watched as his temple began to burn in earnest. "All is transitory, all things illusion." He looked up at Bolan sourly. "Of course this temple was a nine-hundred-year-old illusion that I had grown quite fond of…."

Bolan nodded. "I'm glad none of the brothers were killed."

"Yes." The abbot heaved a heavy sigh. "That is a blessing."

"Gather up your people." Bolan turned to Lily and Nyin. "Tuck pistols under your robes but lose the rifles. You're both still monks until further notice. Go down the mountain with the abbot and his people. Your cover should still hold. I'll link up with you when I can."

The abbot nodded. "Assuming we are not detained, tortured and killed, I will take your people to the temple in Lonton. It is not far from here, and on the southwest shore of Lake Indawgyi. Your people will find sanctuary there."

Lily was not happy with the idea. "But, Cooper, what about you?"

"There's still a chopper in the sky." Bolan began gathering weapons. "And there's a shooter on the ground."

THE SHOOTER WAS GOOD. He had nearly taken Bolan's head off twice. The Israeli Tavor rifle was one of the most accurate assault rifles right of the box and came standard with an optical sight. On the other hand Mack Bolan had his scout rifle back in his hand, and he'd engaged in a decade-long love affair with the weapon. He found the blood trail that told him he'd wounded his opponent.

Bolan crouched as the treetops above whipped and tossed in rotor wash and he caught a glimpse of bright yellow and orange as the black-skinned Hind passed over. A doorgunner occasionally rattled off a burst, but he was firing for effect.

Bolan raised his voice as the chopper pulled away. "You want to negotiate?"

A deep Punjabi-inflected voice shouted back from somewhere back in the trees. "I am always pleased to negotiate with a friend and ally of my country!"

Bolan figured that was too reasonable coming from a man he'd just shot. His opponent was also most likely full of it. "The

Burmese army is going to be here any minute. Why don't you extract? I give you my word that I will ask my government to share the information with you."

The Indian called back chidingly. "Do you truly wield such influence?"

"Yeah, I do."

Bolan's opponent took a moment to consider that. "I believe you are sincere, and yet I believe that this information would be shared out to my government piecemeal, and only at great cost and concession."

Bolan didn't bother to deny that what the laptop contained was one hell of a bargaining chip. "I could give you one million *kyat* as a personal concession!"

"Most generous!"

"Or I could just shoot you again," Bolan shouted.

This was met by a moment of stony silence. "Why don't you just walk away?" the Sikh counteroffered. "Leave the laptop. It will also be in my nation's best interest to share the information it contains."

Bolan checked his watch. "I can walk all the way to Laos if I have to, and you're running out of time."

"Very well, my friend. I propose this. Summon the woman and your local ally from hiding. Come with me into my helicopter. You may retain your weapons. We will fly to a neutral country, say, Bangladesh. We can both have teams from both our respective nations meet us there. Whereupon we will make a copy of the hard drive and then go our separate ways in peace and friendship."

It wasn't a bad offer, and Bolan's first instinct was to trust the man. India would be able to pour overwhelming force into the sparsely inhabited eastern border of Bangladesh, but if the CIA scrambled they could put enough people in place that there would be an international incident of biblical proportions if the deal went sour.

Bolan's eyes went to slits as he spied the helicopter in the distance through a break in the trees. A fast rope was dangling from the side of the chopper. Bolan did a little math. A Hind could carry eight passengers in its crew compartment. He'd taken out four on the railroad tracks and lobbed a grenade into the cabin. The doorgunner had stopped firing. Bolan raised his optical sight. The doorgunner was nowhere to be seen. That told him the man had deployed and there was no one left in the cabin to reel the rope back up. Bolan had been busy talking, and the big Sikh had put a man behind him. That did not necessarily negate the deal. "What if I tell you I don't have it on me!"

"I am afraid I may have to verify that myself!"

"I'm afraid I'm not willing to subject myself to a hard-drive cavity search!"

"That is unfortunate," the Sikh shouted. "What must I do to prove my sincerity?"

"Tell me who's been vectoring you in."

"I am afraid I do not have the clearance to do such a thing."

Bolan played his last card. "You tell me who was tracking Miss Na's movements and mine? I'll give you the hard drive, straight up! Then my government will negotiate with yours for a copy, at cost and concessions chosen by India."

"Your government will never agree to that!"

"No," Bolan conceded, "but I will."

"A deal?" the Sikh considered. "Between yourself and I?"

"My government can't afford to have a mole giving away our most sensitive special operations. Your government can't afford not to get China's latest generation of ballistic missile technology. It's not a bad trade." Bolan decided to play his hunch, as well. "As a gesture of good faith? I'll tell you now that if your doorgunner takes one more step I'm going to blast his head off."

Bolan waited to see if his bluff would work.

The big man back in the trees shouted back urgently. "I have ordered him to withdraw fifty meters!"

Bolan tried to gauge whether he was being counterbluffed, but he couldn't detect any movement on his flank.

"I must contact my superiors," the man shouted.

"We're out of time," Bolan shouted back.

"I must—" The man was cut off by the sound of an explosion above. Black smoke smeared the sky. The helicopter's engines were making terrible, off-kilter noises, and as it limped into view Bolan could see that something had smashed into its starboard exhaust duct. Dozens of flares shot out from both sides of the aircraft as the pilot deployed his antiinfrared countermeasures. A streak of fire shot up from the foot of the mountain, and a second missile hurtled upward unerringly and slammed into the Hind. The huge helicopter's nose dipped as its engines failed and it lost lift. The chopper went into autorotation and began its death spiral toward the valley below.

"That didn't come from my people," Bolan roared.

A rifle fired a burst behind Bolan. The Indians didn't care. Negotiations were over, and they had to take what they'd come for and start walking. The flanker was charging, trying to flush Bolan from his position. He'd heard Bolan's bargaining exchange with his officer and had a good idea of Bolan's location. So did his commanding officer, and a grenade thudded to the soil at Bolan's feet. The soldier recognized the British-made M-84 flash-stun weapon. He'd used them many times before. He'd been on the wrong side of them, as well. The blinding flash temporarily overloaded every photosensitive cell in the retina. The sound blast disturbed the fluid in the inner ear and temporarily destroyed the sense of balance, as well as deafened the victim.

Bolan didn't leap from his cover. Instead he dropped his rifle on its sling and covered his eyes with his hands and plugged his ears with his thumbs just as he'd done during the blast at the train. Bolan still saw orange behind his hands, and the concussive crack of the sound wave hit him like a slap but he was not blinded, deafened or unbalanced. He instantly shouldered his rifle and fired as the flanking man came loping through the trees. The man spun in midstop as if someone had hit him with a hammer, and he tumbled out of control into a tree trunk.

Bolan rose and rifle fire cut through the trees inches above his head. He took three running steps and leaped behind the tree with the fallen man. The big American had holed him through the shoulder, and he stared up groggily and brought his hands before his face in panic as his adversary loomed over him. Bolan wasn't interested in taking his life. He stripped the Indian soldier of his satellite phone, then ran through the trees with his prize. He could hear the Indian officer reach his soldier. He had a wounded man on his hands and the chase was over. The sound of attack whistles rising dimly from the foot of the mountain told Bolan a new chase had just begun.

He punched buttons as he ran. Aaron "the Bear" Kurtzman answered on the first ring. "Striker!"

"Bear! The Indians are definitely in play. Have just engaged and breaking contact. Do you have satellite on northern Burma?"

"We've watching 24/7 waiting for you to make contact."

"Good." Bolan gave Kurtzman the coordinates to the temple. "I'm on the western face of the mountain. The temple is on fire, and I think the Chinese dropped the Indian chopper. Burmese patrols are swarming up in my direction. I need you to vector me past them and off this mountain."

"Copy that, Striker. Switching satellite feed to your location now. Will have intel for you in a few seconds and have an escape route for—"

"No. I don't need an escape route."

Kurtzman was somewhat surprised. "Okay...so what do you intend to do once you get off the mountain?"

Bolan had been considering that. They had a mole problem. It was unthinkable that Stony Man could have been penetrated, but someone had been following Bolan's movements with unerring accuracy. Kurtzman and his team used U.S. military satellites, and a number of people had access to which way they were pointing and even the information being transmitted. Bolan couldn't afford to have a satellite do close-up scans and vectoring him to the temple at Lonton. He'd have to make his own way.

Gunshots sounded in the distance. Bolan paused to press fresh rounds into his rifle and a very bad plan began to formulate in his mind. At the moment a lot of satellites were undoubtedly

scrutinizing the burning temple and the surrounding countryside.
Those he could use.

"Bear, once I'm off the mountain I want you to find me the
enemy main camp and vector me in."

14

Bolan didn't need to be vectored in to find the jungle camp. All he had to do was to follow the screams that were unmistakably the sound of torture. Bolan had passed the burning wreck of the Hind. Something a lot hotter than an antiaircraft missile had done its work, and Bolan suspected either the pilot or the copilot had used white phosphorus to destroy as much evidence as possible.

Bolan wove through the enemy patrols. Now that night had fallen, it wasn't hard. Very few Burmese soldiers were issued night-vision gear. Bolan ghosted among them, sometimes so close he could reach out and touch them. His other advantage was that they were fanning out and sweeping. Bolan was moving toward them right under their nose rather than running. The closer he got to the camp, the less wary they became.

The camp was in a clearing by a dirt road. Parked along the road was a pair of Land Rovers and an old two and half ton military truck. Off to one side, a Panhard armored scout car squatted on its four huge road wheels. Its 20 mm cannon pointed up toward the sky, but its hatches were open, and no one was currently manning it. Half a dozen tents were arranged in a block. One of them was studded with antennas. It was a forward command-and-control camp, but there was no barbed wire or earthworks.

Bolan estimated there was roughly a platoon's worth of soldiers present. Their state of alert was low. The Burmese soldiers were well within government-controlled territory. To them, this was a hunting party, not a war.

They were wrong.

The Executioner had come, and the war was about to get

started in earnest. Fresh screams broke out, and Bolan followed them to the back of the camp. A single sentry stood outside the interrogation tent. He was holding his rifle, but he was much more intent on listening to the screaming and questioning going on inside than defending the camp from invaders. Bolan only had two magazines for the silenced pistol, so he drew his blades. The screaming covered the sound of Bolan's approach. He snapped the tomahawk over the sentry's shoulder and yanked back. The bottom edge of the blade cut off the man's shout. The sentry's body stiffened as Bolan's knife slid into his kidney to the hilt. Bolan withdrew the blade, then slit his throat and dragged the sentry a few feet into the darkness. He moved back to the tent and peered through the flap.

An Indian officer sat tied to a chair. His turban had been knocked from his head, and his long black hair spilled across his shoulders. A bloody field dressing lay on the floor beside him, and fresh blood leaked down his left arm where Bolan had winged him. His face was bloody and lumped, but that was either an introductory beating or collateral damage from his capture rather than torture. The officer was being tortured by witnessing the torture of his men. The soldier Bolan had wounded up on the mountain lay like a sack of meat to one side and looked as if he'd been tortured with a claw hammer. His dead eyes stared upward, and his death mask was a rictus of frozen agony. A third Indian wearing the shredded remains of a flight suit hung tied between two poles. Subtler methods were being used upon him, and despite being bound hand and foot it took two Burmese soldiers to hold the man while the interrogator worked.

The Indian helicopter pilot screamed as the interrogator slid a long thin needle down through his face. His scream rose to an animal shriek, and he convulsed and thrashed in his captors' arms as the man with the needle found the sweet spot. Facial neuralgia was considered one of the most horrific forms of pain a human being could suffer. It seemed the torturer was using acupuncture needles to stimulate the condition in his subject. The man's muscles rippled like snakes under his skin as the torturer teased the needle and lit up his victim's trigeminal nerve.

The Indian officer roared something in Punjabi and strained against his bonds, but a pair of soldiers held him in place while a third pressed a pistol to the back of his head. He glared pure hatred from under his dark brows. It was very clear he had made up his mind not to talk no matter what.

Bolan took all of this in several heartbeats. He had seen enough.

The Sikh's eyes flared as he saw Bolan step into the tent. He grinned in savage exultation as Bolan raised his sound-suppressed assassination pistol. Bolan ignored the torturers and shot the man holding the pistol on the Indian officer. The two guards holding him gaped in shock and each took a bullet through the brain. The inhuman screams of the pilot covered the noise, and the torturers turned only when the guards collapsed to the ground. The torturers all had pistols, but they were in holsters on their hips.

Bolan shot the two assisting soldiers before they could decide on a course of action. The head interrogator stared down the smoking tube of Bolan's suppressor. Bolan spoke quietly. "Do you speak English?"

The man stared at the muzzle of Bolan's weapon in dread fascination.

Bolan sighed. "If you don't, you're of no use to me."

"I speak English," the man admitted.

Bolan lifted his chin at the man hanging and shuddering in his bonds. "Take the needle out of his face."

The torturer slid his implement out, and the pilot gasped and went limp.

"Now drop it," Bolan ordered.

Instead the interrogator flung the needle like a dart. The blood-stained sliver of steel flew with practiced accuracy toward Bolan's left eye. The Executioner batted the needle aside with his pistol. The man lunged forward with his hands curling into kung fu tiger claws. Bolan snapped his pistol back in line, and it cycled and spit four times before clicking open on empty.

The torturer took all four bullets to the chest, but his palm still slammed over Bolan's heart with bruising force. Bolan punched the muzzle of his pistol forward and rammed it between the man's eyes, and he staggered back a step.

The Indian officer rose up, chair and all, and hurled himself into the back of the torturer's legs in a chop block. The man fell to his knees, and Bolan drove the pistol down into the crown of his head. The torturer's eyes crossed, and he collapsed to join the pile of bodies in the tent. The Indian awkwardly rose to his feet. The chair forced him to hunch, but he was still inches taller than Bolan. His long black hair fell across his face, and he grinned through his beard. "It appears I am in your debt."

Bolan shrugged. "Yeah." He drew his knife and severed the knotted hemp holding the man's hands.

The big man rose to his full height as the chair fell away. He rubbed his abraded wrists and went to a woven basket in the corner of the tent. He retrieved his dagger and a wooden comb and swiftly bound his hair up and retied his turban. He grabbed a small bundle of his belongings and relieved the dead guards of their pistols.

Bolan went to the pilot bound between the poles. He put a finger against his carotid arteries but already knew the answer. "He's dead."

"Of which I was afraid." The big man frowned at the raccoon bruising around the pilot's eyes and the clear fluid mixed with blood leaking from his nose and ears. "He sustained a concussion when his helicopter crashed. I believe the torture was too much for a man who already had bleeding in the brain." The Sikh brandished the pistols in his hands. "But now it is time for you and I to live and serve our countries as best we can. I am Subedar Sikander Singh."

A *subedar* in the Indian army generally commanded a platoon or several platoons. To have achieved that rank in India's highly specialized jungle-warfare units, Sikander Singh would be a decorated veteran and the equivalent of a U.S. Special Forces officer. "My name's Cooper."

"I do not believe you." Singh grinned again. "Nevertheless, I am pleased, too, my friend."

Friend would do.

"You see any monks in this camp when they brought you in?" Bolan asked.

"You mean refugees? From the temple battle? I have seen no…" The *subedar's* smile flashed again and his eyes grew calculating. "I see! You hid your compatriots among the brethren! What—"

"Whatever ideas you have percolating in your brain, you'd better shit-can them ASAP," Bolan warned.

Singh drew himself up again in offended dignity. "If you do not trust me, which is perhaps understandable given the circumstances, perhaps we should each go our own ways. However, I believe an alliance would be helpful."

Bolan stuck out his hand. "Me, too."

"Indeed." Singh took Bolan's hand with visible relief. "Good." He looked around the tent and shook his head. "My communication gear is not in this tent."

Bolan held up the dead man's satellite phone. "I have this."

Singh held out his hand. "It is mine."

"Spoils of war, and I don't trust you that much just yet."

The big man sighed. "Understandable. I shall have to earn your trust, and I must admit my government will not send another helicopter to extract me unless I can tell them the Chinese data is in my possession. Though I may be able to summon aid through our local intelligence network."

Bolan nodded. "Hold that thought." They first they had to get out of the camp.

"I will tell you something for nothing, my friend. My team was indeed vectored in to intercept the train you rode upon, and again we were directed to seek you at the mountain temple."

"I'd gone dark after the train attack. All communication devices were destroyed and abandoned. There was no way they could track us."

"I have found the greatest intelligence asset often lies beneath here." Singh tapped his turban. "Perhaps your enemy is very shrewd."

"Yeah, our enemy is well aware of our limitations."

Singh looked dubious. "*Our* enemy, my friend?"

"The air-to-air missiles that took your Hind totally ignored its decoy flares and infrared countermeasures. That tells me they were Chinese QW-3s. Just about every shoulder-launched air-to-air missile in the world is a heat seeker. The QW-3 uses a laser seeker. It paints its target with its own light and arrows straight in. That makes it expensive as hell, particularly in a man-portable weapon. No way Burmese troopers would have any."

"Yes, and even Chinese infiltration troops would be most unlikely to deploy such a weapon in Burma, unless of course someone had informed them that a gunship optimized for infiltration had been deployed by their rivals." The Indian officer looked at Bolan appraisingly. "You are very shrewd, and we do indeed have enemies in common. Going dark, as you say, is perhaps our current, best option."

Bolan jerked his head toward the tent flap. "Who's in the camp?"

"Burmese light infantry. A smart unit, well equipped and disciplined. I believe the search for you and your companions is being directed from here."

"Anything else of interest?" Bolan asked.

"Well, I find it of interest that for such a small troop concentration, there are two captains. I suspect that one is a Chinese infiltration officer."

It wasn't a bad guess.

"Well, I thank you for rescuing me, but I do not think we can afford to dally. Shall we make our escape?"

"You're welcome, but it wasn't a rescue mission. You just got lucky. I came here to do some damage."

"I see." Subedar Singh considered the pistols in his hands. "I believe we are outnumbered approximately twenty-five to one. A tactical retreat might prove wisest."

"Can you drive an armored car?"

"Indeed." Singh's beard and mustache split in a smile that could sell toothpaste. "I can drive an armored car."

"So let's have some fun."

"You may have some fun." Singh knelt beside the bodies of his men and snapped off their dog tags. The big Sikh was no longer smiling. "But you will forgive me if I take revenge."

Bolan nodded. "Payback's good, too."

The two men crept from the tent and crouched in the dark as they spied a soldier sitting on the steel fender of the armored car. Singh waved a hand at Bolan and stalked forward. The Burmese soldier started as a black-turbaned, raid-suited figure nearly two feet taller than he was appeared out of the dark and yanked him off the armored vehicle. Singh spun the man and snaked his arm around the light infantryman's throat. The Sikh put a giant palm against the back of the soldier's head and shoved savagely. There was a pop, and the soldier sagged.

Breaking a man's neck wasn't as easy as most people thought. Bolan had done it, and it wasn't easy at all. Even if you knew one of the several techniques, it took a combination of great speed and strength.

Subedar Singh had made it look child's play.

He took up the man's rifle, folded the stock and then folded his immense frame into the cramped driver's position of the armored car. Bolan clambered up top and dropped down through the hatch into the turret. The vehicle was a French-made Panhard AML with a 60 mm breech-loaded mortar and a 20 mm cannon. A .30-caliber machine gun was pintle-mounted on top. For its size, the Panhard packed a hell of a punch.

"Are the keys in the ignition?" Bolan asked.

Sikander craned his head back from the driver's position and peered up into the turret. "It is a push button. It has a approximately three-quarters of a tank of petrol. Tell me when you wish to begin."

Bolan checked his weapons. The Giat 20 mm automatic cannon had a 50-round belt of ammo in the box. He slid a 60 mm high-explosive mortar bomb out of the rack by his shoulder and locked it into the weapon's breech. "Don't turn her over, but give me power to the turret."

"That will drain the battery very quickly," Singh cautioned.

"I know. But I want maximum surprise."

Singh flicked switches below. "You have power."

"Get on the .30."

Singh clambered up past Bolan and stood up in the hatch.

Bolan pulled on his control toggle, and the turret whined as it swung around and the 20 mm cannon lowered. The advantage of the French Brandt mortar in this installation was that it could arc fire through the air like a regular mortar or engage in straight-line direct fire like a cannon. Bolan put the mortar's sight on the tent with all the antennas on top and pushed the trigger. Pale yellow fire geysered out of the 60 mm mortar's maw, and the AML rocked on its chassis with recoil. The command tent billowed violently and rose up in the air like a thirty-foot canvas ghost borne on a cushion of fire.

The .30-caliber machine gun rattled into life in short bursts as Singh targeted the sentries on the perimeter. Bolan slammed open the smoking breech and slid in a fresh mortar bomb. He put his sight on the next tent and fired. Orange fire exploded into the night. Men around the cook fire twisted and fell as machine-gun rounds reaped them like wheat.

Bullet strikes sparked and whined against the welded steel hull as someone returned fire.

"Sikander! Button up and get this heap rolling," Bolan shouted as he reloaded.

The Indian officer dropped down into the turret and slammed the hatch after him. He folded himself into the driver's compartment, and the AML shuddered and spit blue smoke into the night as the diesel turned over. "Which way?"

"Ramming speed."

"So be it."

Gears ground, and the Panhard lurched onto the dirt road and rumbled toward the camp. Small-arms fire was coming hot and heavy, and it sounded like hail on the hull. Bolan looked for muzzle-flashes through his armored periscopes and cut loose with the 20 mm cannon. The high-explosive rounds detonated like giant orange firecrackers everywhere they hit. Bodies burst like water balloons, and tents withered and collapsed. The largest tent was a barracks, and men were spilling out of it.

Singh drove the armored car straight into it. Tent ropes snapped, and the heavy canvas fabric dropped down on bunks and the struggling lumps of men.

Subedar Singh ground them all down beneath the huge road wheels and left a flattened death shroud behind him stained with blood and tire tracks. "Behind!" roared the big man. "Left! Left! Left! RPG!"

Bolan yanked his toggle and the turret turned with agonizing slowness. The Panhard was designed to resist small-arms fire and shell fragments. An RPG rocket would crack its armor like an egg and turn the inner compartment into a kiln of molten metal and superheated gas. Bolan abandoned the turret controls and hurled open the turret hatch. He stood up and swung the machine gun around on its ring mount.

The rocketeer had dropped to one knee and was leveling his launch tube.

Bolan squeezed the trigger of the machine gun and held it down. Tracers streamed from the machine gun and walked up the man's chest as if they were climbing his ribs like a ladder. The rocket motor fired, but at the same time one of Bolan's bullets hit the football-shaped warhead, and the rocketeer and his loader disappeared in a pulse of fire, smoke and shrapnel.

Bolan scanned for more support weapons, but the survivors were fleeing for the trees in all directions. One tent still stood, and he dropped back down into the turret and reloaded the 60 mm mortar. The mortar thumped, and the tent went up in flame. Secondary explosions blasted and cracked, and Bolan knew he'd hit the spare RPG rockets and probably the antiaircraft missiles, as well.

The Executioner swung the turret back around toward the little car park and cut loose with the 20 mm cannon. He held down the trigger button, and first one and then the other Land Rover flew apart into their smoking and twisted main assemblies. The belt of high-explosive ammo fired its last round. The cannon popped and ticked, and Bolan could feel the heat radiating from it. He threw the dual feed lever over and went after the Burmese deuce and a half with the armor-piercing incendiary.

The truck didn't blow up like the jeeps or the tents, but the cannon shells chewed fist-size smoking holes through the engine and cab as if some titanic sewing machine had broken its moorings. The tires exploded under the assault, and the smoking truck sagged to port like a ship run aground.

Bolan surveyed the carnage. He would have liked to scout around for some intel, but the fleeing soldiers would not have gone far, and once he left the armored car all advantage would be lost. Bolan called down into the cab of the Panhard. "Sikander!"

"Yes, my friend?"

"Let's do some distance."

15

Captain Phyu stared in shock at the shattered, burning remains of his command camp. Half of his men were dead and more were wounded. His communications suite had been obliterated. He was one of a minority of Burmese officers who'd had access to a modern computer network, and this was going to be very hard to explain to his superiors. The captured Indian officer was gone, and no useful information had been extracted from him. Every vehicle in camp had been destroyed.

All except one.

Captain Phyu watched as the taillights of his personal command Panhard disappear down the dirt road. A few of his men had collected the wherewithal to fire at the escaping vehicle, but the bursts from their submachine guns and automatic rifles were like the buzzing of flies against the rolled-steel hull of the AML.

In an eye blink his armored car turned around a curve in the road and was gone.

Captain Dai rose up shakily out of the shrubbery. The only thing left standing was the interrogation tent. He had been in it moments before, and only the need to relieve himself had saved him from the slaughter. He entered the tent pistol first to find Khoay-Peng and his Burmese assistants assassinated and his Indian rival and counterpart gone. He came out to find Private Su standing to one side. The sniper had survived the onslaught, but his rifle's barrel was twisted at a strange angle from the stock where the armored car had run over it. He looked at his commanding officer with a helpless shrug.

Dai knew with absolute certainly who had done this. It was the white devil. The American. If the American and the Indian had formed an alliance, then so be it. It would simply help him kill two birds with one stone. Captain Dai looked at Su and knew exactly the kinds of stones he needed to bring his birds down. Playtime was over. He was going to need helicopters and sniper teams.

Before he had been reluctant to ask Variance for help. That reluctance was now gone. It was the time for the son of a bitch to earn his pay. "Su!" Dai snarled.

"Yes, Captain."

"Gather up our surviving men." He turned to his ally. "Phyu."

Phyu stood staring at the burning tents and his blasted and crushed men.

"Captain Ohnmar Phyu!"

Captain Phyu's head snapped around. "Yes, Captain Dai."

"How many sniper teams does Nagar Company have?"

"Four!" Phyu responded. "We have four teams. They are currently deployed with the search groups."

"They have failed to find the enemy. However, the enemy has found us. Order the return of the search teams. I want your sniper groups and helicopters to bear them. My man Su will require a new weapon. The enemy cannot go far in their stolen vehicle. With the rising of the sun we shall hunt them."

Phyu was too shocked by the evening's events to object to Captain Dai giving commands. Indeed a part of him was grateful that someone was taking action. "I shall arrange for it immediately."

"Excellent." Dai stared down the dirt road. "Su!"

The sniper snapped to attention. "Yes, Captain."

"Find me some communication gear that works." Dai shook his head. The question of the day was which way had the American and the giant Sikh gone?

BOLAN AND SINGH ROLLED through the night in their new ride. Bolan had given the Indian his night-vision goggles to drive by and told him to cut the headlights. Bolan stood up in the turret by the machine gun and watched the countryside roll by beneath the light of the stars. The breeze of their passage was a pleasant respite from days of marching beneath the sweltering sun and creeping through stifling humidity. He was reluctant to give up the little armored car, but come the dawn when Burmese gunships filled the sky, it would stick out like a sore thumb and the steel box would become their coffin.

The big man below seemed to read Bolan's thoughts and shouted up to the turret. "We must abandon this vehicle soon."

The starlight was enough for Bolan to see the road forking ahead. He rapped his fist on the turret top and Singh brought the vehicle to a halt. The big man clambered out stiffly and stretched. The French designer had not imagined a man of Singh's size behind the wheel.

Bolan looked the big man up and down. He'd had a hard forty-eight hours. "How're you doing?"

"My arm pains me somewhat, but I will not hold that against you." The Sikh let out a long sigh. "I have lost my team. I was captured, and to my further shame it was my men who died under torture before me. I can understand your concern, but I assure you, I am fit."

The Indian officer was tough. "I heard the radio squawking below. You get anything off it?" Bolan asked.

Singh drew himself up in offended dignity. "I give you my word I sent forth no clandestine transmissions."

"I believe you," Bolan said. "I just want to know if you picked up anything."

"My Burmese is limited, and I am afraid you killed my linguistics man."

"Any impressions?"

"Indeed, it is my impression that Burmese military radio is oddly quiet for there having been two battles fought in a pacified area within twenty-four hours' time. Should their radio frequencies not be blowing up, as you Americans say?"

Singh had an interesting point. Burmese radio should be alive with transmissions right about now. But that in of itself told Bolan a lot. "I don't think the captain in the camp has reported in. I don't think Burmese military command knows about your Hind attacking the temple or your capture, much less your escape and the wipe-out of the camp."

"I see. You believe the Chinese and Burmese captains are engaged in a private venture."

"That's my bet."

"It is a good bet, and I concur." Singh looked toward the fork in the road. "So, my friend. Which way shall we go?"

"West." Bolan decided to put his cards on the table. "You guessed right. My friends are dressed as monks. The abbot is taking them to the temple at Lonton. They'll be waiting for me there."

"Ah, by Lake Indawgyi." He gestured at the fork. "Well, we have traveled approximately twenty-two kilometers, and the western road lays that way."

There was no other choice, but Bolan didn't like it. The trip to Lonton was going to take them twenty miles in the wrong direction.

Again Singh read his mind. "You still wish to head for the Thai border, I assume."

Bolan nodded. "Yeah, the closer we can get the more assets I can call upon."

"However, it is the south and west of Burma which are the most heavily populated. May I suggest that we head west? India is less than two hundred kilometers from Lonton. Once we have the data, my government will dispatch a helicopter for us. If you do not wish to risk extraction, the terrain to the west is much easier and sparsely populated. We can walk it if we must, and it will be easier on the woman."

Bolan regarded Singh frankly. "None of those are bad ideas...."

"But you still do not trust me." He sighed heavily.

"No, I trust you. It's your foreign intelligence agency that I'm not sure of. I wiped out half your team. They don't have any reason to love me. To get their hands on the data and then sell it to the United States and Taiwan will be a gigantic temptation. For that matter the woman has been operating in China for some time. The Chinese would dearly love to get their hands on her. Once your government gets everything they want from her, they could use her as a bargaining chip in future negotiations with China."

"Everything you say is true. But they will have to go through me, and I will protect you and the woman with my life."

Again Bolan found himself believing the big man. "Let me ask you this."

Singh glared upward challengingly. "And what would that be?"

"Do you believe I could protect you from the CIA if you had something they wanted?"

Singh looked away and muttered into his beard. "No, no, I do not."

Bolan nodded. "From Lonton, we're walking. Which way I haven't decided yet. You can go your own way anytime."

"I owe you my life, my friend. We are linked by karma. I will follow you and aid you to the best of my ability. You had best get down now."

Bolan hopped down while Singh clambered in through the driver's door. He cranked the wheel and drove the AML straight into the underbrush by the side of the road. The jungle seemed to close around the armored car's path and swallow it. Any decent tracker would be able to detect its track during the day, but from the air Bolan doubted anyone could notice. A few moments later Singh emerged. He had the government-issue Uzi that had been racked by the driver's compartment and six spare magazines slung across his back. The roof-mounted machine gun lay tilted casually across his shoulder with a belt of ammo locked in place and a reload draped over his chest like a full-metal-jacket shawl.

Bolan and Singh took the western fork in the road and started walking.

MARCHANT WEIGHED EXPOSURE and risk against the biggest payday of his life. He had to get his hands on the Chinese data, and all that was standing between him and several extra zeros in his checkbook was one off-the-books paramilitary spook. Marchant scanned his scanty data for the thousandth time. That wasn't quite true. He pulled up the file on Subedar Sikander Singh. Despite Marchant's bigoted opinions of people from the Indian subcontinent he had to admit Singh was one serious soldier. The unknown American was another. And there was the little local shit, Nyin. Plus a Taiwanese agent who belonged in a top-end Hong Kong brothel rather than the jungles of Burma.

It shouldn't be this hard.

Marchant ran the sequence of events in his mind again. Captain Phyu and his men had captured Singh and the remnants of his team, and it was clear they had been in a battle and obviously that battle had been with the American. The commando had escaped, but the strange thing was there had been no sign of Nyin or Na. Somehow those two had slipped off the mountain during the fighting. The question was how did you sneak one of planet Earth's arguably most beautiful women past seasoned mountain troopers scouring the mountainside?

Marchant instantly knew the answer.

You hid her in plain sight. You had a firefight on the mountainside with soldiers swarming up toward it and monks scattering down like chickens out of a burning temple. All it would take would be a couple of saffron bedsheets and a straw hat, and the dumb Burmese bastards would probably have actively assisted in giving them safe passage. So they had separated. Nyin and Na had escaped down the mountain while the American had fought the Indians and won, and then in a fit of cowboy-type bullshit he had rescued Sikander Singh.

Marchant smiled sardonically at his screen.

Not quite bullshit. Between them the American and the Indian had cleaned Nagar Company's clock and scampered off in an armored car. But where had Nyin and Miss Na gotten off to? Probably not any village. Money was already well spread to report anything suspicious, even dressed like a monk the woman would not be able to withstand close scrutiny and once she opened her mouth the jig was up. Another temple would be their best bet. The question was where? Hopin and Lonton were the two closest towns of any size. Both were in pacified territory.

Military raids on the temples would go over like a French kiss at a family reunion. For that matter, Marchant still had it in the back of his mind to retrieve the data by his own means and jack up the price to all buyers. He needed the temples searched, and that was something most Burmese would balk at. Marchant didn't need soldiers or policemen on this one.

He required scum.

Marchant picked up his phone and dialed a number. It was time for his old friend and favorite scumbag U Than to make himself useful again.

16

Lonton Temple

Abbot Ba-Maw did not look particularly pleased to see them. He stood on the temple steps with the abbot of Lonton and Nyin. The two monks stared at Bolan and Singh, probably wondering if they'd come to blow up this establishment, as well. Nyin glared up at the giant Sikh and was clearly hostile. "No!" He shook his head at Bolan. "Oh, hell no!"

Singh ignored the little Burmese agent and turned to Ba-Maw. He pulled a thick wad of rupees from his pocket. "I am afraid it was I who destroyed your temple. I cannot replace any of your religious antiquities, but please accept this small token to help with the repair."

"I thank you." Ba-Maw reluctantly accepted the cash and tucked it into his robe. He and the other abbot exchanged a few words. Ba-Maw gave Bolan a hard look. "This is Abbot Htut. He regrets the fact he cannot give you sanctuary. He will not risk his temple any further. You may spend the rest of the night here, but before the dawn you must take the woman and go."

"Tell him I understand." Bolan said. "Where's Lily?"

Nyin continued to give Singh the stink-eye. "She not doing so good."

"Is she hurt?"

"No, trip to Lonton temple uneventful. Thumb ride on army truck. But she no Jungle Jane." Nyin waved his hand in a circle that encompassed their situation. "Not her game, Coop."

Bolan nodded. The clubs, casinos and high-rise apartments of Hong Kong, Bangkok and Beijing were Lily's battlefields.

Nyin jabbed a thumb back at Singh. "Why you hanging with him?"

"He's with us, Nyin," Bolan stated. "Get used to it."

"He blow up train. He blow up temple." Nyin waved his arms up and down. "He almost kill us."

"Yeah, he's a talented guy. We need him." Bolan leaned down and locked eyes with Nyin. "And if you can't you hang with that, walk. You've already done your bit. No hard feelings."

Nyin scowled ferociously but turned on his heel and said nothing. Bolan followed him into the temple and found Lily in a small monk's cell. She sat curled in a corner. A bowl of brown rice lay uneaten to one side. Every few moments she ran a hand across the glossy black stubble where her waist-length locks had once hung and winced in misery. Lily Na was a spy, a seductress and an assassin. Bolan could only imagine what acts she had committed and what atrocities she had endured. Having her head shaved appeared to be the worst indignity. She glanced up as Bolan entered the cell and flung herself weeping into his arms. "Take the data! Just take it and go! I will only slow you down! I will stay here! I will take the orders of a nun! I will…I will…" Her knees buckled as she wept inconsolably.

Bolan made soothing noises and let her cry.

Nyin glared at Singh to let him know this was all his fault.

Singh tsked in sympathy and shook his head. Like their men, once baptized, Sikh women never cut their hair. To see a beautiful woman sheared so saddened him down to his soul. He brightened and held up a finger. "Here, perhaps I may be of assistance." He reached into his pack and pulled out a length of folded black cloth. "If I may be so bold?"

Lily stared red-eyed at the cloth and with a little sob inclined her head. Sikander Singh swiftly wound the cloth around her shorn skull, then stepped back and examined his handiwork proudly. "Behold! You look like the very queen of the Punjab!"

The Sikh had wound Lily a turban. She touched the black fabric covering her stubble. "I shall wear it proudly, thank you," she said.

"You are most welcome." Singh smiled at Nyin smugly.

Bolan shrugged. "Told you he was a talented guy."

Singh unslung the Uzi and held it out to Nyin. "Here, I have brought you a present."

Nyin grumbled but took the weapon and its six spare magazines.

Bolan helped Lily to her feet. "We've got a few hours to get some shut-eye. I suggest we take it."

Nyin and Singh eyed each other warily and left the cell. Bolan turned to go but Lily clutched his arm. Her huge dark eyes stared up into his pleadingly. "Please…stay."

BOLAN AND LILY LAY in each other's arms. Her turban was somewhat askew, but laying naked among the saffron robes, beneath the flickering light of an oil lamp in a stone cell with one of Nyin's black cigarettes filling the room with the smell of cloves, she truly did look like some mythological queen of the Far East. She had spent the past four hours exposing Bolan to her mastery of the art of seduction.

Their interlude was interrupted by the sound of vehicles outside the temple. The temple itself was just outside the town and overlooked the lake. It didn't get much traffic on Tuesdays, much less at 4:15 a.m. Bolan rolled to his feet with the Chinese assassination pistol in hand and peered out the tiny window of the monk's cell.

Lily pulled a pistol out of her small bundle of belongings. "What is it?"

"Trouble."

A sedan and a minivan were pulling up to the temple with their lights off. Four men got out of the car and another eight from the van. Bolan brought his night-vision goggles to his eyes and powered up. The approaching men wore off-the-rack tropical suits, smoked, spit and approached in a loose mob. They didn't act like soldiers on a raid. They carried a hodgepodge of the cheap Chinese-made knock-offs of Western pistols that flooded the Asian black market.

They were thugs, pimps and thieves.

Bolan had a good idea who had sent them.

Sikander Singh stuck his head in the door. "Men come."

"Wake up Nyin."

"I have. He is ready."

Bolan grimaced as two of the twelve thugs broke off and began wandering around toward the back of the temple. "Tell Nyin we've got four men heading around. We can't have any of these guys reporting back. We have to take them all quiet and quick."

Singh loosened his kirpan dagger in its sheath. "Quiet and quick."

Bolan took pistol and tomahawk in hand. The Lonton temple was much larger than the one on the mountain. The building surrounded a courtyard with the main temple hall front and center. A wing of cells for the monks to dwell in flanked one side, with a kitchen and storerooms on the other.

Bolan blew out the lamp and crept out of his cell. The goons were already in the temple grounds. He heard robes rustle behind him and knew that Lily had his six. Shouting broke out in the courtyard and flashlights clicked on in the gangsters' hands. Gunshots rang out, but the bad guys were simply firing their weapons in the air. Bolan pushed Lily back into their room as a detachment of five goons broke off and entered the dormitory. They kicked in doors, fired their guns and shone their flashlights into the faces of the blinking and terrified monks.

Bolan and Lily had shared the last cell down. Bolan waited within as the thugs spread themselves out along the dormitory hall and brutally kicked and shoved the monks toward the courtyard. One of the gangsters came down the hall and kicked open the door. He stopped cold as he took in Lily standing against the wall. Too late he saw his executioner standing to one side. Bolan yanked the man into the room, sunk his tomahawk into his skull and ripped his weapon free.

The Executioner strode out into the dormitory hall. He had to avoid casualties among the monks, which meant he had to prevent the firefight from breaking out as long as possible. Bullets had a tendency of going through people, and the monks and thugs were mixed close in the hall. He was going to do his work up close.

Two gangsters were forming a rear guard as they gleefully booted monks along in the opposite direction. Bolan stepped up behind them and capped one in the back of the head. The small noise of the suppressed pistol was covered by the shouting and gunfire. The second thug caught the motion and spun about. Bolan sank his tomahawk in the man's stomach and gave him one to the temple as he folded.

Several monks goggled back at Bolan, but they flinched from the smoking gun and bloody blade in his hands as he pushed his way through the mob. Bolan reversed the tomahawk in his hand and leaned over a monk to take a textbook tennis forehand swing. The gangster never saw it coming, and he went limp as the tomahawk's back spike penetrated the base of the brain. Another gangster saw Bolan out of the corner of his eye but was too late to evade the blow. Bolan's tomahawk stabbed down behind his collarbone and hooked him like a fish. The man screamed, but lots of people were screaming and yelling. Bolan yanked the smaller man in and slammed the muzzle of his pistol beneath the gangster's chin. Brain and blood geysered up through the crown of the man's head.

The last gangster pinned Bolan in his flashlight beam. Bolan raised his pistol, but the man shouted and crouched in the mob of milling monks. A huge dark shape dropped down behind him from the rafters. The man opened his mouth to scream but a huge hand clapped over his mouth, and then a kirpan dagger opened his throat from ear to ear. Several monks howled as they were showered with arterial spray.

Sikander Singh shoved the dead man away. "I make that five."

"Plus two in back and five in the courtyard." Bolan's math was the same. "Where's Nyin?"

"He is crouching behind the Buddha, with the machine gun."

Bolan nodded. That wasn't a bad place for him. "We've got about a heartbeat before the bad guys figure out something's wrong." The problem was the monks. There seemed to be at least thirty in residence, and more than a dozen had already been ushered into the courtyard. The remaining monks milled around and clutched one another, and neither Bolan nor the big Sikh spoke Burmese.

Singh drew his Hi-Power pistols and rose to his full height, extending his arms until the muzzles touched both sides of the hallway. He started marching forward milling his arms in big circles as if he were herding chickens.

The monks got the message scattered before him back to their cells.

"How many rounds have you left?" the Indian officer asked.

"Four."

The pistol in the Sikh's left hand twirled and he presented it to Bolan butt first. "Here, take one of mine."

"Thanks." Bolan checked the loads and moved forward. Lily came forward and the three of them crept out into the courtyard. Over a dozen monks were in the courtyard, but the good news was their captors had them kneeling with their hands behind their heads. The exceptions were the two abbots. Abbot Htut was on the ground clutching his split scalp, and a grinning gangster loomed over him with a revolver that was bloody from the pistol-whipping.

Abbot Ba-Maw stood with remarkable stoicism as the apparent leader of the gangsters opened his coat and drew out a ten-inch chef's knife wrapped in newspaper. He put the point beneath Ba-Maw's chin and said something that made his men laugh. He threw his own head back to laugh just in time to take Bolan's tomahawk in the teeth. The knife fell from his hands and he staggered back spitting teeth and bubbling blood past his newly cleft palate.

The goon with the revolver raised his weapon, but Singh hammered him down with a 3-round burst. Bolan raised his own pistol and snarled as a number of the monks rose and bolted in all directions waving their hands. He roared at Ba-Maw. "Tell the brothers to get down!"

The abbot shouted above the turmoil, but the monks were overcome by panic. Some of the monks from the dormitory actually ran back out to see if they could help. Bolan found himself in the middle of a Buddhist fire drill, but unlike him the gangster scum didn't care about collateral damage. A monk screamed and fell clutching his arm as he took a bullet meant for Bolan. Singh swore a mighty oath in Punjabi and held his fire. Another monk gasped and fell as he took a bullet between his shoulder blades.

There was no room for courtesy. Bolan threw monks down to bring them out of the line of fire as he advanced across the courtyard. One monk had actually stopped and was trying to pull Abbot Htut to his feet in the middle of the firefight.

"Coop!"

Bolan turned as Lily ran past and tossed him her pistol. Bolan caught the weapon in passing. She flew into the two monks' legs and took them down like a pair of bowling pins wrapped in bedsheets. Her selfless act also cleared a line of fire. Bolan instantly took the opportunity and targeted a Burmese gangster. The thug staggered back with his pistol firing high and wide as Bolan printed twin patterns in his chest.

An automatic weapon snarled from within the temple itself, followed by the bark of pistols. Bolan instantly knew that was Nyin's Uzi and the two men out back were rushing in. The Uzi snarled a second time, and Nyin's voice rose above the din. "Coop! One got past—"

The temple door flew open and a thug ran out with pistols barking in both hands. He aimed one back blindly into the temple and fired the other into the courtyard wildly, apparently not caring if he hit Bolan's team, the monks or his own men. Bolan and Singh fired at the same time, catching the man in a cross fire and sending him tumbling down the temple steps.

The two remaining gangsters dived for a pair of huge painted clay pots destined to grow ornamental trees. Bolan fired his pistols and ceramic shattered. Soil poured from the holes, but two or three feet of earth was one of the best bullet stops in the world. The two men snaked their pistols over the top and fired blindly. One pistol snaked back, and Bolan's instincts told him the man was clawing for his cell phone.

Bolan's voice shook the courtyard. "Fatso! Fire support!"

Nyin crashed through the double temple doors. The FN MAG machine gun he bore was nearly as big as he was.

"Jars! Jars! Jars!" Bolan shouted.

Nyin grasped the situation immediately. He stopped at the temple steps. Two guardian Buddhas framed the door, and he dropped the muzzle of the MAG across the starboard Buddha's knee. The general-purpose machine gun cycled into life. The clay shattered, and the dirt within erupted as he held down the trigger on full-auto. The .30-caliber rifle rounds tore apart everything before them, and the cowering criminals screamed as bullets tore through their cover and turned them into corpses. Nyin stayed on the trigger until the last round was spent. He dropped the smoking machine gun to the steps and whipped out his pistol.

Bolan strode through the shuddering, weeping monks. The two gangsters lay twisted among the potting soil and ceramic shards. He picked up a cell phone and checked its screen. They'd gotten lucky. A preset number was up but had not been dialed. They would have a little time before someone expected the temple raiders to report in with what they might have found.

The courtyard was quiet other than the moans of the wounded.

Abbot Htut suddenly lurched to his feet as he became aware of the fact that he was entwined with a beautiful woman. Bolan moved to the temple gates but the gangsters had left no drivers in the cars and nothing moved. It was a clean sweep. Bolan turned back to find Singh and Nyin seeing to the wounded. "How bad is it?"

Three monks appeared to be down with gunshot wounds. Singh was tearing saffron strips from a robe and trying to staunch the bleeding on both sides of a monk's body. "This one has been shot through the lung. He will require immediate medical attention."

Abbot Htut stood clutching his bloody scalp with one hand and shaking his fist at Bolan.

Ba-maw translated. "The abbot says you must leave immediately."

Bolan nodded. "You take the minivan and get the wounded to the hospital in town. We'll take the sedan and go the other way."

"There is no other way," Ba-Maw said. "The road ends here in Lonton. The only other way to go is west, toward India or north toward China on foot. Either is still a very long walk."

Neither option sounded good, and Bolan was getting tired of walking. The enemy had the Burmese army and police, Chinese special forces and the entire Burmese underworld at their disposal. Walking out of Burma was just too much exposure time. They had to get out of Burma and they had to do it now. "Abbot, does Lonton have an airstrip?"

"I do not know." Ba-Maw turned to his counterpart and they exchanged a few words. Ba-Maw shook his head. "Abbot Htut says no, but he says there is one in Hopin."

Bolan and Singh had passed Hopin on their way to the lake. It was ten miles back. At four-thirty in the morning traffic would be light, but what traffic there was would probably be military and looking for them. It was a risk they'd have to take.

"You have a plan?" Singh asked.

"Yeah, but not a good one."

"Oh?"

"We burn for Hopin. We steal a plane, and we get the hell out of here."

17

Hopin Airfield was military, but was little more than a dirt field and incapable of supporting jet aircraft. They had made the ten-mile journey to Hopin in record time and ditched the car a mile outside the city to avoid any checkpoints. Bolan and his team were forced to skirt the town in a wide circle until they located the airfield, which had eaten some time. Bolan had hoped to get out under the cover of darkness, but now the sky was just starting to turn orange over the mountains.

The airfield was surrounded by storm fencing and had a gate with a guard box. A prefabricated hut doubled for both the flight shack and the control tower. The flight hangars consisted of several arcs of somewhat rusty corrugated iron, and parked near them was a fuel tanker truck.

Sikander Singh squatted by his side. "Have you chosen?"

Bolan eyed their possible rides.

A pair of ancient-looking Russian Mi-2 helicopters squatted on packed clay pads. He saw a twin-engine Cessna, but what drew Bolan's eye was a camouflage-painted Pilatus PC-6 Turbo Porter. The single-engine Swiss prop plane was nicknamed "the jeep of the air" and with good reason. It was as tough as hell, operable from the worst of landing strips and had one of the shortest takeoff and landing runs of any small plane extant. The Porter could land in the space of less than a soccer field and had an enviable reputation for floating when ditched.

Bolan nodded toward the Porter. "That one."

"I see." Singh pointed toward a hut. "But there is a guard at the gate, and a light on in the shack."

Bolan was loath to kill a gate guard or some hapless wing-wiper in the shack. The shack was fifty yards away. The guard was facing their way, but his attention was taken up with spitting betel and reading a newspaper. Bolan doubted he or Singh would be able to sneak up on him. "Nyin, I want you to take the guard, but take him alive. Walk up bold as brass."

"Right." Nyin frowned. "How?"

"Take my pack, walk up and then kick his ass."

"Right!" Nyin had left his monk's robes behind and now wore a pair of khaki pants and a T-shirt the monks had scrounged up for him. He tossed Bolan's pack casually over his shoulder and started walking up to the shack. The guard failed to notice him until he was ten feet in front of him. The guard stepped out, but his hand never went close to his pistol. Nyin spoke to him for a minute and pulled out a pack of cigarettes. The guard nodded and dug in his pocket for a light. Fifty yards away Bolan could hear the smack of the flesh as Nyin sucker-punched the unsuspecting gate guard.

Bolan broke into a run. "Let's go!" He charged across the open ground with Singh at his heels. Nyin was tucking the crumpled guard into his box as Bolan and Singh hurdled the gate. The two commandos sprinted for the shack. The plywood door flew off its hinges beneath Bolan's boot. A startled man in a flight suit nearly knocked over the tea he was brewing on a hotplate.

Bolan rammed the muzzle of his 9 mm into the man's belly and then drove the butt into his kidney as he folded. Three dumb-struck men sat around a folding table playing cards. The man in the middle started to get up, and Singh's leg lashed clear across the table and sent him flying backward. In a feat worthy of a yogi the big man retracted his leg and stomped the folding table in two. He shoved a pistol into the face of the card player to his right and his kirpan rang like a bell as it cleared its sheath and flipped beneath the chin of the other. The two horrified men sat in their chairs with their cards drooping in their hands.

Nyin and Lily ran in with guns leveled. Bolan pointed at the card player beneath Singh's knife. "Nyin, ask him if there's any-one else on the airfield."

Nyin grinned and had a quick conference with the man. "He's mechanic. He say there no one else except guard. I take care of him."

"Yeah, I saw. The Pilatus Porter, what's its status?"

"He say he work on it yesterday. Leaking a little oil but otherwise say it fueled up and tip-top."

"How soon are they expecting company?"

The mechanic balked, and Singh's kirpan parted the uppermost layer of flesh of the man's throat. He gulped and fired off a stream of Burmese. Nyin nodded. "He say it scheduled for reconnaissance mission up north at 1100 hour."

Bolan checked his watch. It was not quite six o'clock yet. That would be a good five-hour head start, and they would need every second of it. "Tie them up."

Singh and Nyin began hog-tying the airfield personnel. Bolan walked to a corner of the shack that was fenced off and padlocked. He looked at the military green crates and the two hand trucks within. "Nyin, ask him if that Porter has hardpoints."

Nyin prodded an answer out of the mechanic. "He say five. Two on each wing. One on centerline."

Bolan shot the lock off the cage. "Sikander."

"Yes, my friend?"

Bolan considered the crates. "I'm going to need your help manhandling some ordnance."

"THEY HAVE ESCAPED!"

Marchant noted the rising tone of panic in Captain Dai's voice. He was aware of the early-morning battle at Lonton temple and the slaughter of the local street muscle. However, even in failure it had served a purpose. The sacrilege had galvanized the local police, as well as the local Burmese underworld. Police checkpoints were everywhere and an informant or a knife lurked in every alley. Their only option was to start walking through the woods again, in which case Dai and his sniper teams would resume the hunt, but that in of itself would not have Dai so agitated. "How have they escaped, Captain?"

"They made it to an airfield in Hopin. They stole a plane."

Marchant felt panic of his own suddenly rise. "How long ago?"

"At dawn. We were lucky that a delivery truck arrived around nine and found the gate guard tied up. Otherwise we would not have known until noon."

Marchant's fingers flew across his keyboard. "What kind of plane?"

"What?" There was a sudden flurry of Mandarin on the other side of the line. "A Pilatus Porter."

Marchant opened a map window of Burma on his computer. Hopin was a little over one hundred miles from the Indian border. He did a quick search and pulled up the PC-6's specs. It was a light utility-transport, single engined with a cruising speed of 161 miles per hour at 10,000 feet. The Burmese plane was undoubtedly old and had seen heavy use. Marchant estimated it could go 130 at full throttle and the American would be hugging the deck to avoid detection and flying around mountains rather than over them. Call it one hundred miles per hour average. The math was still ugly.

The data was in India by now.

Except in that case Marchant would have heard about it. His Indian contacts would have told him the job was over and smugly informed him he would not be receiving the back end of his payment. So the data was still in Burma, and the American most likely still in the air. Marchant calculated. To the north and east lay China. The only way to go was south, but where? He could be in India right now and be safe, relatively. The American clearly did not trust his ally or wish to be interrogated by Indian intelligence.

So where was he going? Marchant's eye traveled down the long border with India and stopped. There, at the westernmost tiny corner of Burma, was the border with Bangladesh. Marchant smiled.

Neutral ground.

Marchant calculated times and distances.

"The American is heading for Bangladesh. He must be intercepted. Captain, the national security of the People's Republic of China will depend on how speedily you can arrange this."

Dai's voice went professional. "I will see to it at once."

"Good, has Captain Phyu assembled his sniper teams and requisitioned the helicopters to transport them?"

"Yes, but why—"

"Get yourself and them in the air as quickly as possible and get them heading south at emergency war speed." Marchant leaned back in his chair. "We may need a little insurance."

BOLAN CROSSED the Tropic of Cancer at noon and their luck was still holding. He glanced at the map on his knee and adjusted his course a little more westward. He could see the Chin Hills approaching and beyond them would be Bangladesh.

Lily looked back and forth between Bolan and Singh. "What will happen to me in Bangladesh?"

Bolan glanced at his gauges. "I figure it this way. We get to Bangladesh and make two copies of the data. One for Sikander's government and one for mine. Then you keep the laptop and the original. I guarantee you I will put you on a plane to Taiwan. After that? I don't know, maybe…a yoga retreat in Costa Rica?"

Lily smiled like the sun.

"Bandits!" Bolan roared. "Ten o'clock!"

It had been too good to last. Bolan rammed his throttle full forward and the turboprop roared in response. A pair of helicopters swept toward them clearly on an intercept course.

"Mi-2s!" Sikander Singh had sharp eyes. Luckily the two lumpy, oblong little Polish helicopters were wearing civilian paint and markings and didn't have the weapons pylons on the sides to mount Russian 57 mm rocket pods or automatic cannon. However, the doors and windows had been removed and the muzzles of automatic weapons stuck out of the sides like the spines of a violent hedgehog.

"Nyin, Sikander, get on the doorguns." Bolan yanked on the stick to bring the Porter into a steep climb. It would be much harder for the men in the helicopters to shoot up than down and they would risk shooting through their own rotors. "Lily, give them fresh belts as they need them."

Singh and Nyin clambered back into the cabin and slammed

open the Pilatus's large sliding cargo doors and locked them
open. Both men shrugged into the chicken straps that would keep
them from falling out of the plane. The munitions cage back at
Hopin airfield had been small but well equipped. Bolan had an
FN MAG machine gun to port and starboard, as well as a minigun
pod on his port wing and a twelve-tube rocket pod to starboard.

The Pilatus was known for its maneuverability, but no plane
could turn and burn at low altitude and speed with a helicopter.
Indeed a helicopter didn't even have to engage in traditional
dogfighting; it could spin on its axis to continually keep its guns
on target, and unfortunately the Pilatus wasn't a speed demon.
The Mi-2 could match Bolan horsepower for horsepower.

However, Bolan did have them outgunned, and he had been
in dogfights before both as gunner and pilot. He was betting
whoever Chinese intelligence had rushed behind the stick three
hours ago in Burma weren't combat pilots, either. Bolan flew
straight toward the starboard chopper. A couple of shooters stuck
pistols out the windows and took potshots as Bolan and the
chopper screamed toward each other at closing speed.

Bolan waited until they were close and squeezed his trigger.
The Porter vibrated as the minigun's six barrels spun into life
at 4,000 rounds per minute. Tracers streamed into the nose of the
oncoming chopper, and it was nearly occluded by sparks. The
pilot pulled out of the line of fire. Bolan rammed his stick down
and dived, but the helicopters dipped their noses and dropped
down like stones for the intercept. Bolan yanked his stick back
up and climbed, but the choppers rose up like dragonflies as they
came to grappling distance.

As Bolan passed between the two helicopters, the Pilatus was
raked by shotguns, submachine guns and automatic rifles from
both sides. Bullets sparked across the nose of the plane. Bolan's
windscreen cracked, and a bullet smashed out his side window
and tore through his headrest. Bullets screamed through the
fuselage and crossed through the cabin.

Nyin and Singh fired back with their MAGs. The firing pass
lasted less than a second, but red lights lit up Bolan's console.

"Nyin!" Lily screamed.

Bolan risked a glance back. Nyin had been blasted to pieces. He hung in his chicken straps like a badly dressed side of beef. His eyes were rolled back in his head and his mouth hung open. His machine gun rattled in its mount abandoned. Lily pressed a hand to his throat and shook her head helplessly.

Nyin was gone.

"You can outclimb them," Singh shouted. "They are helicopters. Their ceiling cannot be much more than four thousand meters. Ours must be triple that. Climb for the clouds!"

Bolan grimaced. Singh didn't have a bad idea except that if they flew much higher than a thousand feet they were going to light up any Burmese air defense radar like Christmas. The Burmese air force was undoubtedly irked that someone had made off with one of its planes that morning, and would most likely scramble something the little Porter wouldn't be able to outrun.

Or simply shoot it out of the sky.

Behind him the helicopters had already spun around to give chase. Bolan was losing power and needed enough lead to turn.

"Lighten the load." Bolan commanded. "Chuck Nyin's gun and everything else that isn't nailed down."

Lily pulled out the clip holding the MAG to the door mount and heaved the weapon up and out the door. She looped one belt over her shoulder and then pushed the box of spare belts out the window, as well.

Singh unclipped from his straps. A Porter could carry up to ten passengers. The Sikh swiftly uncleated the back two rows of seats and hurled them out the door. They gained a little speed but the helicopters swiftly gained. There would be no room to turn and when he did the choppers could turn their guns on them. There was only one choice left. "Grab on to something!"

Bolan yanked the stick all the way back. The airframe of the Pilatus groaned, and Lily screamed as the plane went into a full-throttle loop the loop. The chopper pilots panicked and split apart as Bolan came diving into them upside down. Bolan triggered the rocket pod beneath his wing, and six white-phosphorus marking rockets rippled from their tubes. Two of the rockets were chopped in two and exploded by the whirling steel rotor blades but four passed through to strike the chopper. Three exploded against the side of the fuselage, and the fourth flew through an open window and detonated inside. The entire helicopter filled with white smoke and fire.

"He falls!" Singh boomed triumphantly. "He falls!"

Bolan had no time to savor his victory. He leveled out of his loop and put himself in the chase position on the remaining helicopter, which had dipped its nose and was pulling away under emergency war power. Gunmen leaned out the windows and fired their weapons wildly. Bullet holes chewed their way across the nose of the Pilatus, and more warning lights came on across Bolan's board. Slowly but steadily he was losing power. Bolan wanted to get close before he fired his last six rockets. He flipped over his trigger switch and held it down on the minigun.

Bullets screamed across the chopper's starboard side. Several of the men leaning out the windows jerked and flailed as they were hit and fell limp in the windows with their bloody limbs flapping. Bolan jinked the Porter and was rewarded as sparks erupted around the chopper's tail rotor. The minigun spun dry but the damage was done. The helicopter slowed as it yawed and the pilot fought his collective.

Bolan roared in and loosed his last six rockets at point-blank range. All six projectiles slammed into the rear and tail of the chopper. It lost all power to its tail rotor. Bolan veered off as the stricken burning helicopter began its death spiral toward the ground. They had won but the price was high. There wasn't warning light on his board that wasn't blinking and he was swiftly losing visibility as oil spritzed out of one of the bullet holes over the engine. The bullet holes began spewing smoke as the oil caught fire.

They weren't going to make it to Bangladesh.

"Strap in!" The stick was sluggish as Bolan took the Pilatus into a long slow dive and looked for his landing strip.

Singh pointed downward. "There!"

Bolan squinted past the oil smudging his windscreen. The Indian officer had spotted a paddy. It was not ideal, but the water and soft mud would cushion the impact, which beat the hell out of smashing the plane through the trees. "Hold on!"

Bolan eased back on his throttle. He almost didn't need to the way he was losing power. The big American brought the Pilatus down to just above stalling speed as the rice field rushed toward them all too quickly. Bolan pulled back on the stick and the airframe jolted as it hit the water. The plane dragged its tail for a moment and then the landing gear hit. Water sprayed up in all directions. The plane lurched as if the earth had grabbed it as the wheels hit mud. The nose dipped and rammed into the mud. Only Bolan's straps kept him from flying through the windscreen, and they tried to squeeze his lungs out of his chest. The Pilatus stood on its nose and slewed about before slamming back down.

Bolan groaned and clicked out of his harness. Smoke oozed into the cockpit from the oil fire still burning in the engine and Bolan could smell gas. "We gotta go!"

Singh's turban was askew and blood streamed down his face from his split eyebrow. He ignored his injuries and turned to Lily. Her face was white with shock and her left forearm hung at an awful angle. "Her arm is broken. Get her out while I fetch the weapons and gear. I fear we will have to leave Nyin. His was a noble death."

Bolan unbuckled Lily. She gasped as he lifted her out of her seat and carried her to the cabin door. "Can you walk?"

She nodded shakily. "Yes…I will walk."

Bolan gingerly lowered her down into the paddy. He jumped down as Singh tossed him their scant belongings and dismounted the remaining doorgun. Smoke poured from the engine compartment. Singh jumped down and the battered trio moved away from the smoldering plane. Lily cringed as it whooshed and caught fire. They squelched through the mud and clambered up on to a foot path.

Lily made a little noise and fainted dead away.

Singh knelt beside her and shrugged philosophically. "It is probably for the best. The arm requires setting immediately."

"Yeah." Bolan reached into his bag for his medical kit. It was sparse in the extreme but he did have a field dressing, as well as antiseptic and some painkillers. The Sikh cradled Lily as Bolan went to work. Bone and gristle scraped and she made a slurred unconscious noise as Bolan put the bones back in place. He unscrewed the flat plastic legs of his scout rifle's bipod and splinted the arm.

Singh nodded approvingly. "You have done this before."

Bolan nodded. He'd done it far too many times before, including on himself.

"So." Singh stared up at the Chin Hills. "We walk."

"Yeah, we're walking." Bolan stared at the black smoke rolling up into the sky like a billboard announcing to the world where they were. He figured it was forty miles to the border of Bangladesh and a lot of that real estate was vertical.

18

Stony Man Farm, Virginia

Aaron Kurtzman stared at the map of Burma. Mack Bolan had gone dark since the battle at the mountain temple. There was no new intelligence. The only intelligence Kurtzman had to work with was his own. The good news was that his intellect was formidable. He sat in his wheelchair as still as stone, staring up at the giant plasma screen on the wall and ran the variables through his head for the thousandth time. It was very likely that Taiwanese intelligence had been penetrated. By the same token, the Taiwanese had spies deeply imbedded in the mainland.

However, none of that would explain the battle on the railroad. Neither the PRC nor Taiwan would invite a third player, much less Indian intelligence, to the party. Bolan had gotten out of that one by the skin of his teeth, yet, though he had destroyed the transponder and gone dark, still the enemy had tracked him.

Someone had vectored the Indians in a second time to hit the mountain temple. Someone had hooked up the Chinese with U Than. NSA communications satellites were monitoring all relevant military and police frequencies, and it appeared someone had ordered local drug muscle to attack the temple at Lonton at four in the morning. The gangsters had been annihilated, and Kurtzman doubted it was the monks who had been operating the light machine gun. Now it appeared an airstrip at Hopin had been attacked and a plane stolen. Kurtzman smiled grimly. Bolan hadn't gone completely dark. He was leaving his calling card everywhere he went. The smile died on Kurtzman's face. That was the problem. If he could connect the dots and follow Bolan's trail so could his opponent. There was someone, somewhere, sitting in a room much like the Farm's War Room and staring at a screen just like he was.

That someone had tipped off the Chinese, the Indians, Burmese armed forces and the Burmese underworld. Someone was playing all sides against the middle, and they were doing it for profit rather than the national security of their country. Both Indian and Chinese intelligence would be feeding him data from their satellites and their spy networks on the ground, but Kurtzman just wasn't buying that being enough to explain all that happened. He had no proof, but by the pricking of his thumbs he knew with terrible certainty that someone had been looking at the same U.S. satellite reconnaissance pictures and intelligence data streams that he had.

Whoever was orchestrating this dog-and-pony show was an American.

Kurtzman punched his intercom. "Carmen?"

Carmen Delahunt immediately answered. "Yeah, Bear. I'm trying to figure out Mack's possible flight plans now. I'll have a list of viable destinations for you in about five minutes."

"Belay that for the moment. Tell me, how many satellites do we have observing Burma right now?"

"Right now it's priority one. We have seven on-line and the NSA is moving an eighth into position."

Kurtzman sighed. He pretty much knew the answers to his questions and none of them were good. "How many people would have access to the satellite streams?"

The vivacious redhead was a former FBI agent, and she could see where this was going. Her voice sounded as if she had tasted something unpleasant. "We have a mole."

"I believe so. On our side."

Huntington Wethers walked over and stared at the screen. "I heard the last bit of that. You and I are thinking the same thing." Wethers was a former professor of cybernetics, and his logic was second to none.

"That we have a mole?"

"Right," Wethers confirmed.

"And?"

"And we've got India, China, Burma all in the mix? Man, this guy's connected. He's seen, predicted or found out about Mack's every move."

Kurtzman shifted in his wheelchair. "So?"

Wethers shrugged. "So let's assume he knows about Nyin."

"Hunt, I had David McCarter call in a favor with MI-6 to bring in Nyin when Mack told me he thought there was a leak. Not even the Pentagon knows about Nyin. The only way the asshole could know about Nyin is if either you, me or David leaked it." Kurtzman frowned. "And I'm not buying that. So how could he know?"

"My point exactly. Let's assume he knows about Nyin and reverse engineer it."

Kurtzman saw it. "He figured out Mack was getting help from someone local, but he couldn't find any U.S. or Taiwanese assets in play."

"And what other kind of under-the-table asset could Mack call upon in a former British colony?" Wethers lifted his chin at Kurtzman's secure phone. "You need to get David on the horn with MI-6. See if anyone had made any inquiries about Southeast Asia that could include Nyin's operational purview. The request was probably made casually, by someone well trusted by MI-6, and couched in drug interdiction strategy rather than the current crisis."

Kurtzman nodded appreciatively. "Not bad."

"YOU SAY THE PLANE IS DOWN?" Marchant leaned back in his seat. "Were there survivors?"

Captain Dai shouted above the sound of rotors on his end. "There are three villages in the valley. Many of the locals watched the dogfight but luckily none of these villages has electrical power or phone service. So far only we know of the air battle and we are bribing the villagers to keep it that way."

"What about the woman and the laptop?"

"The plane was burned out when we found it. The body of

Nyin, the MI-6 asset, was inside. We must assume the Na woman, the *subedar* and the American commando are still alive and armed."

"What about your helicopter teams? Why haven't they apprehended them?"

There was moment of stony silence before Dai responded, "Both helicopters were shot down. All hands on board both aircraft were lost. However, their path is plain. They have gone into the Chin Hills and are making for the border of Bangladesh as you predicted."

"What is your force disposition?"

"Between myself and Captain Phyu we have three sniper teams, one of my own and two of his. Between his forces and mine we have three sections and two helicopters."

"How are you deploying?"

"One sniper team and one rifle section has already begun tracking. The other two will leapfrog ahead and deploy along their most likely route into Bangladesh. The helicopters will act as airborne spotters."

"Excellent."

"However, as you said before. I believe we will require some… insurance."

Marchant frowned. "Oh?"

"Yes, the American has proved elusive before. It would be best if there were a welcoming committee waiting for him across the border."

"I'm sure your government can arrange something."

"My government does not wish to provoke an international incident. My government thinks that perhaps it is time you took direct action."

"I'm on it," Marchant agreed.

"You…will take care of this personally?" Dai's tone was one of surprise.

"My boots are on the ground. Assuming this all goes off according to plan, it will be my privilege to buy the first round of beers in Dhaka."

"I…" Dai was dumbfounded. "I will inform my government."

"Way ahead of you. I'll contact you again when my team is in place. We'll be positioning at the southern end of the Chittagong Hills. Keep me abreast of anything that develops on your end, especially if the commando changes course. I will stay on the Bangladesh side of the border as a surprise unless you call for direct interdiction, agreed?"

Dai didn't like hearing it, but they both knew the plan was sound. "Agreed. Contact me when you are in place if I do not contact you first."

"Variance out." Marchant considered his next course of action. The commando had finally taken a casualty, and it was going to cost him dearly. Without Nyin he had no native Burmese speaker and no way to receive refuge in a village or temple except at gunpoint. He had only one option, and that was a death march for Bangladesh.

Marchant decided he would indeed go to Bangladesh. He had exposed himself far too much on this deal, but the rewards had already been astronomical. He was a multimillionaire from what the Chinese and Indians had already paid him for his services, but now it was time to seal the deal and get the hell out of Dodge. If all went according to plan, he himself would apprehend Miss Na, kill the American and then sell the data to the Chinese, the Taiwanese and the Indians. With a little fancy footwork, he could probably expect a hefty check from Uncle Sam, as well.

Marchant opened his office closet. He took a small remote out of his pocket and punched in the combination to the concealed safe room. A section of wall hissed back in its tracks to reveal a small cubicle. He went to the racks along the wall and chose his old favorites. The Heckler & Koch submachine gun gleamed like new, and he had recently added an electronic Aimpoint sight. He took down a load-bearing vest and inserted six loaded magazines into the pockets. He smiled as he checked the action of his 10 mm Smith & Wesson. He loaded it and tucked it into the vest's built-in shoulder holster along with a reload. Marchant pulled out a drawer removed a much scratched and abused Gerber Mark II fighting knife. It was a very distinctive dagger.

Marchant's father had carried this knife in Vietnam, and while Marchant was an excellent shot he had done the majority of his wet work with the blade. He strapped the knife in place on his vest upside down over the left chest strap for ease of draw. Then he reached into his pocket and took out the most deadly weapon in his arsenal. Marchant punched a preset number in his cell phone, and a voice answered on the third ring. "Yo, Variance, what's up?"

"Tito, you want to go to Bangladesh?"

"Bangladesh?" Tito sneered in disgust. "Fuck no."

"You want a hundred grand?"

"Damn straight!"

"You've got half an hour to find someone who speaks Bengali."

"I got just the person in mind."

"Good, see you in a few. Variance out." Marchant put his gear into a long aluminum case and stepped out of his office into the CIA's tertiary Bangkok office. His secretary looked up at him happily from her desk. "And where are you going with that smile on your face, Tom?"

Marchant hefted the case and rattled the contents. "Fishing. I'm due."

19

Bolan looked up at the sound of rotors. He recognized the make immediately. They were Bell UH-1s coming in hard and fast.

"I count two," Singh said.

They crouched beneath the forest canopy as the Hueys thundered over and continued westward. Bolan took a long hard look at Lily. Her arm was splinted, he'd given her morphine and they'd used the turban Singh had given her for a sling, but she was far from all right. Nevertheless she held her Browning Hi-Power pistol cocked and locked in her good hand as the sound of the choppers receded to the west.

"Perhaps they are not looking for us," Singh suggested hopefully.

All three of them knew that was wishful thinking. Looking back from the crest of the last hill they had crossed, Bolan had seen their pursuers. The enemy was leap-frogging men ahead of them. Once the teams were deployed, the helicopters would take to the sky as spotters.

Singh shrugged. "We are not covering our tracks effectively, and given our currently circumstances I do not believe we can. These Nagar Company soldiers have jungle-craft skills perhaps equal to our own. I cannot think of any way to throw them off our trail. They will be radioing ahead which way our trail leads to those who lay before us. They will vector them in, and they will close in from all sides."

"What are you suggesting?" Bolan prompted.

"I suggest I go back along our trail and kill as many of our pursuers as I can. Perhaps this will give you and Miss Na the chance to slip through the cordon ahead."

It wasn't a bad idea, except for the fact that it was suicide, and Bolan wasn't buying. "I've got a better idea." Bolan considered the terrain they had crossed. "Let's go back about a kilometer and a half to that ravine we passed and kill all of them together—how'd that be?"

The *subedar* breathed an honest sigh of relief. "To be honest, I do find your plan preferable."

"If they're smart, they'll have deployed snipers with their pursuit teams. I think we can take most of them in the ravine, but we'll have to watch out for the sharpshooter hanging back." Bolan took Lily by her good arm and eased her down under a moss overhang and handed her a canteen. "Stay here. Rest. We'll back in a little while. With any luck these bastards will have brought our lunch."

Bolan had expected she might break down weeping and beg not to be left alone. Instead the Taiwanese agent quirked one eyebrow. "Hmm…Burmese army rations. I cannot even begin to imagine what culinary wonders await."

The Burmese army usually lived off the land when they were on maneuvers, which meant taking food from the mouths of any villagers they came across. However, Nagar Company was an elite unit, and with any luck they had been issued something vaguely fit for human consumption. None of Bolan's team had eaten since a scant bowl of rice and pickled vegetables back at Lonton temple.

Bolan rose and nodded to Singh. "Let's go meet the lunch wagon."

The War Room

"THANKS, NIGEL, CHEERS." David McCarter hung up the secure phone with MI-6 and grinned at Kurtzman in victory. "We've got the bastard! Nigel is sending us the information now."

Kurtzman sagged back into his wheelchair with relief as information began scrolling across his screen. The first thing was a photo ID of a strikingly handsome man in a suit. He vaguely looked like an older, more heavily built version of Brandon Lee, the actor son of kung fu legend Bruce Lee. Unless one had been told it was hard to tell the man was Eurasian. Kurtzman had seen the man's photo before. Indeed, the Farm had used him as an intelligence asset in the past. Kurtzman's fingers flew across his keyboard as he brought up data. The man's record was heavily redacted, but it was enough to know that he could mastermind a situation like this.

Thomas Marchant, age thirty-seven. He was the son of Jonston Marchant, who had been a Green Beret in the Vietnam War. During the war he had fallen in love with a Vietnamese woman named Mei Mui. After the fall of Saigon, he had stayed in Asia and become a CIA paramilitary officer.

Marchant and Mei had a single child, Thomas Allen Marchant. The boy had grown up a CIA brat, being uprooted and moved from one Asian hot spot to another. He spoke Cantonese, Mandarin, Thai, Japanese and Korean. His friends had been the children of other CIA operators, and like many CIA agents he had taken up his father's mantle. He had literally been raised to be a perfect CIA Asian sector analyst and had risen to a Southeast Asian sector operational controller.

Tom Marchant had spent nearly a decade in U.S. drug interdiction efforts with some spectacular successes. A decade was plenty of time to establish contacts with his opposite numbers in China, and Kurtzman suspected the Chinese had handed many of his successes to him.

Marchant had spent the past few years working as a controller in operations against the People's Republic of China. He had worked hand in hand with the Taiwanese government. Kurtzman could only imagine what secrets Marchant had given up and how many agents had been captured or killed in repayment. He had also developed contacts with both Indian and British intelligence, as well as the intelligence agencies of most of the east Asian nations. It had put him in a unique position.

The position to reach out his hand and take the next generation of nuclear deterrent from the world's new Communist superpower.

It had also put him in the loop to use NSA satellite feeds of Southeast Asia. Kurtzman shook his head and grimaced as data continued to spool down a separate window in his giant screen. The CIA had actually been using Marchant to help in organizing ground efforts to locate and assist Miss Na. Just about the only thing he didn't have was a blueprint of Stony Man Farm.

Kurtzman smiled grimly and punched a button on his console. "Barb, I need you to get in touch with the CIA Bangkok office. I need the station chief to take Marchant out of play. Consider him armed and very dangerous."

"I'm on it," Price confirmed.

BOLAN CAUGHT MOTION at the entrance to the ravine. He pushed off the safety of his rifle as a downpour hammered out of the sky in sweat warm sheets. "They're coming."

"Indeed." Sikander Singh lay prone behind the MAG machine gun on a shrub-covered hillock looking down into the ravine. He ignored the drenching rain and kept his eyes fixed on the fire zone.

"Two bursts, three at most. Then move," Bolan cautioned. "If they have a grenadier, he's going to light up this position."

"Indeed." Singh never took his eyes off his sights. "Then you shall similarly illuminate him."

"With luck." They were going to need it. Bolan was down to his last two grenades. His scout rifle had served well, but breaking through the cordon that lay between them and Bangladesh was going to take firepower—firepower they were going to have to acquire the hard way. Bolan took his shooting position farther down the hill and waited.

The point man came into view. He wore a Burmese uniform and carried a Galil assault rifle with a 40 mm grenade launcher attached. The weapon was definitely on Bolan's shopping list. The ravine formed a natural part of the trail. The point man was wary. He knelt and looked at the trail and then the walls of the ravine that were a few feet taller than he was. He motioned back, and two soldiers climbed the walls of the ravine and began cutting trail on either side of it through the thick brush. The point man slowly made his way forward, once more scanning the hills beyond and the mud beneath his feet for traps.

Bolan and Singh held their fire, waiting for the body of the unit to enter the killing box.

The point man exited the ravine and came to the foot of the hillock. He turned back and gestured to men who were out of sight. Five more soldiers came into the ravine. One was carrying a rocket launcher, which was also on Bolan's shopping list. If Bolan were in command down below he would have another grenadier and a sniper with the section. Those men would form the rearguard and hit back hard on anyone who attacked the main body.

Bolan could feel them in his bones. Somewhere unseen just beyond the ravine. They were waiting.

Singh cut loose as the men reached the middle of the ravine. It sounded like giant sheets of canvas tearing as he sent strings of fire into the ravine. The Burmese were caught flat-footed and had no cover to run to. They twisted and dropped as the MAG shredded them. The point man swung his weapon toward the chattering machine gun above him. Bolan put his crosshairs on the man's chest and fired. The heavy subsonic slug slammed the man into the mud.

Back beyond the ravine a grenade launcher thumped, but the MAG already fallen silent as Singh abandoned it. The big man literally slid down the muddy rain channel down the side of the hillock like an escape chute. Bolan hadn't seen the grenadier's flash, but he was pretty good at judging tube noise. He raised his weapon for a high arc and the scout rifle bucked against his shoulder as the grenade launcher fired. Automatic fire chattered in the trees overlooking the ravine as Bolan announced his position to the flankers.

Singh's Uzi coughed in three quick bursts, and one of the flankers tumbled forward over the lip of the ravine. Mud erupted in geysers inches from Singh's position as the other flanker sprayed for payback.

Bolan slid his last frag into his launcher and fired. The trees and shrubs at the top of the ravine shuddered as the grenade detonated and sent a shock wave of jagged metal shrapnel in all

directions. A bloody hand flopped into view out of the greenery
and twitched a few seconds before curling into a death claw.

Bolan was already sprinting down the hillock for the dead
point man. He slung his scout rifle and seized the Galil and
pouches of magazines and grenades. The rear guard grenadier
had not fired a second time. That meant Bolan had gotten lucky
or the grenadier and the sniper were clawing their way up their
own hillside for higher ground. Between the pouring rain and the
thick undergrowth Bolan couldn't find them. He shouted over the
downpour as he flipped up the grenade launcher's ladder sight.
"I can't see them! Fire for effect!"

Bolan had probably just signed Singh's death warrant, but the
subedar charged down the ravine, scooped up a dead man's rifle
and began spraying bursts blindly up into the hillside. A high-
powered rifle cracked in response. Singh's turban ribboned away,
but the skull underneath appeared to be untouched. Bolan hadn't
seen the flash but Singh obviously had. He took deliberate aim
and emptied his rifle in a long burst. The sniper rifle in the trees
cracked a second time. Blood flew in a red mist down in the
ravine and Singh staggered.

Bolan saw the muzzle-flash. It was a straight shot sixty yards
away. Bolan leveled his weapon and fired. He didn't wait for the
detonation but fought for traction in the muddy hillside to pull
himself parallel with the sniper. He caught movement through the
trees and rattled off a burst from his rifle. Bark erupted from a tree
trunk to Bolan's right as the sniper responded, but his aim was off.

A rifle cracked down in the ravine. Bolan had no time to look
down, but the weapon was firing steadily on semiauto. Bolan
rattled off another burst and his weapon ran dry. He dropped the
rifle and drew his pistol, firing as he came on, and saw that the
sniper was trying to put a tree between himself and the rifle fire
below, as well as shield himself from Bolan. The Executioner
fired his pistol as fast as he could pull the trigger and closed to
thirty yards. His pistol ran dry at twenty, and he dropped the spent
weapon and filled his hands with cold steel.

The sniper rose up from his position and leveled his weapon.

The tomahawk flew from Bolan's hand and revolved through the rain. The sniper instinctively, and fatally recoiled from the flying weapon. His muzzle went off target as he flinched and his shot went wide. The tomahawk sank into the tree trunk by his shoulder. The sniper tried to bring his weapon back on-line, but Bolan was already upon him.

The sniper screamed as Bolan raised his knife. The scream was cut short as the serrated steel plunged down behind the sniper's left collarbone and touched his heart. The man went limp as Bolan twisted the blade, and the sniper's blood pressure instantly went to zero.

Bolan ripped his weapon free and shouted down the hill. "Singh!"

"I am hit," the man yelled back. "But I am still fit to fight."

Bolan suspected Singh would have said that if he'd had both his arms and legs blown off but for now he would just accept it. Bolan knelt and examined his prize. It was a Heckler & Koch G-3 A-3ZF. Basically a last-generation German assault rifle, but one the manufacturers had tested for accuracy at the factory and then fitted with a scope sight. It was more of a tactical support weapon than a true sniper rifle, but it had higher power optics than Bolan's scout rifle and Bolan needed every meter of reach he could get. He slogged down the hillside and found the grenadier. Bolan's grenade had landed quite close, and the Burmese solider had bled out from multiple throat wounds. The Executioner took his weapon and bandolier of grenades, as well as a fresh pistol. He worked his way down the hill to where Sikander Singh sat against one side of the ravine wall. His long hair fell in a soaked cascade around his shoulders. He held up his left hand and brandished it with a snarl. His thumb had been blown off at the knuckle. "You see this? Now I am most truly and heinously pissed off!"

20

Dhaka, Bangladesh

Tom Marchant stepped into the warehouse and examined his murder squad. Tito "Big T" Tuilosega was half Samoan, half Filipino and nearly three hundred pounds of solid muscle. The sleeveless T-shirt he wore exposed Catholic imagery crawling across his arms in tattoos that went from shoulder to wrist. Beneath his khaki shorts Samoan tribal tattooing entwined his legs to his ankles. At one time he had been a United States Army Ranger until he had discovered much more lucrative employment doing contract work for the CIA and anyone else who could afford his fees. He was not quite a smuggler in his own right and stopped just short of being a paid assassin.

Marchant had used Tuilosega on numerous occasions, both with the blessing of the United States government and on private ventures.

The big man was currently unloading weapons out of a crate and handing them out to a cadre of six Southeast Asian men. They were all barely half his size, but all were muscled like bantam-weight boxers and carried themselves like soldiers. Marchant knew that one of them, Jamanth "Jimmy" Sukarno, had been a member of Kopassus, Indonesia's highly regarded and infamously red-handed antiterrorist unit.

All of them regarded U Than and his thugs with open disdain.

Marchant stuck out his hand. "How goes it, Tito?"

"Real good, Variance." Tuilosega's hand enclosed Marchant's

but stopped short of grinding his bones to powder. He tilted his chin at U Than and his men. "They speak English?"

"A couple of swear words they learned at the movies."

"Cannon fodder?"

"Yup." Marchant glanced at a dark-skinned man checking the optics of his weapon. "That our tracker?"

"Yup, that's Yahya. Smuggling guns through the Chittagong Hills has been the family business for three generations. Yahya, say hi to the boss."

Yahya waved happily. "Hi, boss!"

Tuilosega rolled his eyes. "Once we know where we're setting down, a couple of his cousins will link up with us. Yahya and his boys don't come cheap, but they know the country like the back of their hand, and they don't mind getting their hands dirty, either."

"Good enough. Pay them whatever they're asking and tell them there's going to be a bonus if we hit pay dirt."

Marchant unzipped a nylon backpack, and stacks of tens, twenties, fifties and one hundreds spilled out. "That's for showing up," he said, handing the bag to Tuilosega.

The heavily tattooed man snorted happily at the cascade of cash. "A promising start, Variance." The big man took out a Benelli semiautomatic shotgun and racked a round into the chamber. "Let's get this show on the road."

BOLAN, LILY AND SINGH froze as a pair of helicopters swept over at high speed. The choppers were not doing a search. The tracking team had not radioed in for at least twenty minutes. Bolan and Singh glanced at each other. It was about to hit the fan. The *subedar* jerked his head at him, and the two warriors walked a short distance down the game trail.

Singh frowned at his bound left hand and spoke quietly. "I suggest we split up. You and Miss Na go one way and I shall go the other. I will create a diversion. Perhaps the two of you can slip across the border."

"And the data?"

Singh stared at Bolan steadily. "I will trust you to do the right thing."

This was the second time Singh had volunteered to sacrifice himself for the good of the mission. Bolan shook his head. "No, we'll do better as a fire team than solo acts."

"There is wisdom in what you say," Singh acknowledged. He looked down at their small mountain of weapons. "I fear we must trim some weight."

Singh was right. They had close to two hundred pounds of ordnance and less than three able bodies to carry it. The choices were tough. They both turned as Lily walked up and joined them in staring at the pile. She pointed at the scout rifle. "Your little rifle is light. I can carry it for you."

Bolan nodded. He had only one magazine left of subsonic ammunition, but the ability to kill in silence was too good to give up. He hefted his sniper rifle while Singh slung a rifle with a grenade launcher over his shoulder. They stared at the MAG and the rocket launcher. Both men were thinking about helicopters. Singh sighed heavily. "I have found there are few social situations that an FN general purpose machine gun will not solve, but I believe the rocket will serve us best now."

Bolan agreed. The weapon was loaded and they had two spare projectiles. "All right."

Singh scooped up the weapon and the pack with the spare rockets. "I will bear it. You are our sharpshooter and must remain unencumbered."

Bolan looked at the man appraisingly. In the past forty-eight hours he'd been shot, beaten and had his thumb amputated the hard way. He stood like a man of iron, but beneath the indefatigable strong man exterior the *subedar* had to be at least as tired as Bolan was, and Bolan was weary down to his bones. "We'll switch off. When the fight comes you operate it."

"Fair enough."

Bolan glanced up at the sky. The rain had stopped, and they had about another four hours of daylight. Bangladesh wasn't getting any closer standing around. "Let's move out."

Stony Man Farm, Virginia

"BLOODY HELL!" David McCarter's fist slammed down on the workstation. The CIA Bangkok station chief was apologetic, but he had no good news. Thomas Marchant had stepped out of the office hours earlier, and he had dropped off the face of the planet. Aaron Kurtzman almost never used profanities but he shared the Englishman's sentiment. Thomas Marchant was gone. "We've bloody well lost him, haven't we, then!"

Kurtzman stared at his screen. "Not quite."

McCarter stared but was willing to believe. "How's that, then?"

"Well, where are Mack, Miss Na and the laptop going?"

McCarter saw it instantly. "Bangladesh, the Chittagong Hills."

Kurtzman milled his hands helpfully. "So where is Marchant going if not Bangladesh? In the Chittagong Hills," Kurtzman finished. "Waiting for Mack. Probably with some mercs under his control hoping to intercept the laptop or quite probably take it from the Chinese and then sell the data to all concerned parties."

"Even if Mack can walk out of Burma, he'll be walking into a trap." McCarter stared up Kurtzman's screen. His Phoenix Force colleagues were off duty for some seriously needed R and R. Assembling them would take too long. "Where is—"

"Able Team is on a mission." Kurtzman and McCarter were both thinking the same thing. "And Hal would have to get the President's permission to send them even if they broke the mission."

McCarter stood and stretched. "Right! As an English citizen, I don't have to ask your man in the Oval Office for leave to visit the queen's former colonies, do I?"

"Well…"

"I'm off, then. I expect a private plane, pilot and flight plan ready by the time I hit the airport. Put Barbara on it."

"There's not enough time to get a weapons package put together for you in Bangladesh. We just don't have much in the way of assets in that corner of the world."

"Well, I'll just stop by the British embassy. The guard lads must have something laying about."

"Listen…"

McCarter was already out the door. "When Mack checks back in, tell him I'm on my way and expect to be on the ground in his vicinity in approximately twenty-four hours. Give him a frequency he can contact me on."

21

Bolan scanned through the dusk with the telescopic sight mounted atop his stolen rifle. Singh leaned over his shoulder and spoke quietly. "Do you see them?"

Bolan tracked the hillsides. "No." Nothing was moving except for the fruit bats that were dropping from the trees like autumn leaves in clumps and flapping off for their nightly feeds. Bolan couldn't see anyone. He'd burned the last battery in his night-vision goggles, but again, he could sense the hunters out there. Off in the distance a tiger let out its blood-freezing roar of challenge that echoed across the hills. The big cat knew that other predators were stalking each other across its domain and didn't like it. This night the jungle was ready to swallow up the unwary.

Singh squatted on his heels. His dark eyes tried to bore holes through the forest ahead. "Should we try to pass through them tonight?"

That was what Bolan was considering. None of the party that had been tracking them had been equipped with night-vision equipment, but that didn't mean that the killers ahead of them didn't. "Maybe we won't try to get past them tonight. Maybe we'll do a little hunting instead."

"Oh? And as the prey, how shall we accomplish this?"

"What kind of rockets have we got?"

"I have run a complete inventory. We have three. Two of the rocket grenades are of high-explosive-incendiary-antipersonnel variety, which the Chinese designed specifically for jungle and mountain warfare. I believe the third projectile is an illumination round."

"Fantastic."

Singh leaned in eagerly. "You have a plan?"

"Yeah, you're going to fire for effect."

The *subedar's* expression went flat. "I find your humor swiftly passing the boundaries of good taste."

"Yeah, but I'm not joking."

"I believe you intend to sneak ahead as far as possible. Upon your signal I will fire the illumination round." Singh held up his mangled hand in recrimination. "Then, having announced my presence to the world, you, from a place of safety, will fire upon targets of opportunity while the enemy attempts to slaughter me."

"Great minds think alike," Bolan agreed.

"Yes…so they do."

Bolan shrugged. "If you have a better plan, then—"

"You know I do not!"

"How much candlepower are we pumping?"

"I believe the specifications call for five hundred thousand candles for approximately thirty-five seconds."

It would be enough. "What kind of range we got?"

"If I remove the braking ring and set the timing fuse for maximum, I believe we can get a good fifteen hundred meters."

Bolan pointed into the range of hills. "If they're clever, they're in those hills ahead looking down on us and directly in our way. I'm going to move a little bit south and get on top of that hill just below them and get a little altitude. I'll signal you when I'm in position."

"And what shall this signal be?"

"Three quick pistol shots."

"I see."

"They may mark your launch site and send a hunting party down after you."

Singh rolled his eyes. "The thought had occurred to me."

Bolan drew the silenced assassination pistol and held it out to the *subedar.* "You got four rounds real quiet. Make them count."

"Many thanks." Singh took the weapon and tucked it under his belt. "And what of Miss Na?"

Bolan looked back. Lily had taken off her sarong and in the timeless fashion of Southeast Asia unfolded it and wrapped herself in it like a blanket. She appeared to be asleep. "I'll tell her the plan and I'll leave her your radio. If neither one of us makes it back, she can radio your people and mine and maybe they can arrange an extraction."

Singh let out a long breath. Lily Na was a city girl with a broken arm. If he and Bolan didn't make it back, she wasn't going to last twenty-four hours in the Burmese border country by herself. "I will pray for a miracle."

British Embassy, Dhaka

MCCARTER FOLLOWED the color sergeant into the armory. The Phoenix Force leader was unshaved, unbathed and jet-lagged and by his own admission he looked like something the cat had deposited on the doorstep. But the words "SAS commando" opened doors throughout the UK's former empire, and on top of that MI-6 was keen to see the Chinese data and the CIA agent who had tricked them receive his just deserts. The sergeant waved an expansive but somewhat sheepish hand at the contents of the small room. "Sorry, mate. Don't have much, but what we have you're welcome to."

McCarter stared at the racked rifles with a sigh. They were SA80s, undoubtedly one of the most trouble-plagued weapons of the late twentieth century. They weren't even the latest A2 model that the German firm of Heckler & Koch had been hired to fix. They were the old model. "They're bin."

The sergeant rubbed a horseshoe-shaped scar on his forehead and sighed in sad agreement. "Bin" was slang for "dustbin," which was where most British soldiers believed the SA80 belonged. Embassy guards around the world were generally the last bunch in any military to get the latest and greatest in new equipment. In this one instance that might prove to be in McCarter's favor. "Got anything older, then?"

"Well…" The color sergeant toed a dusty-looking crate beneath the racks. "Might be an old SLR laying about." The two

Englishman produced knives. The box was pried open with a shriek of nails and tearing wood. McCarter smiled happily. There, packed in genuine straw, lay an FN Self-Loading Rifle with a 2X SUIT optical sight.

"I'll take it. What else you got?" McCarter said.

"Got a few LAW rockets…"

"I'll take two."

"Few hand grenades?" the sergeant offered.

"As many as you can spare."

"I was issued a Browning."

"Got me own."

"Bet you have. Anything else?"

"I could use a lift," McCarter said.

"Lift to where, then?"

"Chittagong Hills."

"Might know a bloke with a helicopter who could get you there." The color sergeant scratched his chin. "Who we going to war with, then?"

"Burma and China, mostly."

The color sergeant mulled this over. "Right! You'll be needing food and water."

"For about seventy-two hours, and a medical kit if you can spare it."

"Should be a few MREs and a medi-kit somewhere about. Hold on." The color sergeant wandered back out into the embassy. McCarter took down a cleaning kit from a shelf and began field-stripping the SLR. The weapon swiftly came apart into its separate assemblies, was checked, lubricated and reassembled with the same swiftness. McCarter shot the bolt forward on a loaded round as the color sergeant returned with a bulging knapsack. He sighed at the sight of the gleaming weapon. If it hadn't been finished in matte black it would have sparkled.

"Now that's a fine thing."

"Not a bad piece of kit." McCarter shouldered the rifle. "You said something about a helicopter?"

BOLAN DREW HIS PISTOL around 10:00 p.m. He lay prone at the top of the hill between a pair of large rocks. There was no moon, but there wasn't a cloud in the sky and the starlight alone was almost enough to operate by. The range was long, but his position was as good as it was going to get without exposing himself in low and open ground. He draped a bandanna over the muzzle of the Hi-Power to hide some of the flash and pulled the trigger three times rapidly. He holstered the pistol and dropped behind the sight of his rifle.

Just north of his position a sizzling noise rustled through the hills and a meteor suddenly whooshed upward and into the western sky. Instantly rifle fire crackled from the overlooking hills, and green tracers streaked like laser lines into the smoke and firefly sparks of the rocket launch that hadn't had time to disperse. A light machine gun strobed from a promontory and swept the position Singh had just vacated.

Bolan swung up his sights. The range was close to nine hundred meters, and at night the machine gunner and his loader were dark blobs obscured by the blinding pulse of the machine gun's muzzle-blast. Bolan flicked his selector to full-auto and lowered his aim a hair. He squeezed the set trigger and touched off a 5-round burst. Sparks ricocheted off the machine gun and the dark shape of the gunner flailed and fell.

Up in the sky a star went supernova.

The hills were suddenly thrown into a harsh white acetylene glare. The gunners on the hillsides had emerged from their hides to pour fire down into Singh's position. Bolan flicked his selector back to semiauto. He fired three times, and two men fell back into the bushes while a third tumbled in a pinwheel of limbs down the hill. Bolan scanned for targets as the illumination round swung on its parachute and threw the landscape into surreal landscape of shifting shadow and glare.

Bullets began striking Bolan's position. The Executioner flinched as bits of rock, clods of earth and shreds of shrubbery flew as if the top of the hill were being forced through a woodchipper.

Bolan thumbed his selector to full-auto and fired a quick burst down the hill. A section of riflemen were swarming up Bolan's hill.

Captain Dai had undoubtedly seen the carnage of the slaughter in the ravine and he had set a trap of his own. The hill overlooked the most accessible routes through the hills, and Dai had dropped a team down. They had probably been ordered to let Bolan and his companions pass and then put the cork in the bottle in the valley below.

Bolan had chosen his sniper hide right on top of the hornet's nest.

Rifle and machine-gun fire from the hills ripped into Bolan's position, covering the climbing men and forcing him to stay low. He pulled a Chinese stick grenade from his belt, pulled the pin and tossed the bomb over the rocks. The grenade cracked and was immediately answered by the returning thump of a grenade launcher below. Bolan hugged rock as the grenade detonated just on the other side of his cover. He slammed a fresh mag into his HK and grabbed a fresh grenade.

He was about to be overrun.

Bolan's eyes flew wide as a pistol popped three times rapidly down on the valley floor to his right. Singh was alive, saw his position and had a plan. The lee side of the hill was open and once the enemy crested the top they would cut him down easily as he retreated. Now there was nothing for it. He could hear the shouts of his hunters as they closed on the summit. Bolan tossed the grenade behind him and sprinted down the hill. He flicked the selector of his rifle to semiauto once more and fired off three quick shots into the air as he ran. Behind him the first hunters hit the top of the hill and guns cracked to bring Bolan down.

Bolan threw himself down as a rocket hissed up from the valley floor and literally passed over his head on its way to the hilltop. This was no illumination round. The jungle-mountain warfare munition was a triple threat consisting of nine hundred steel ball bearings bound with two thousand incendiary pellets driven in all directions by a half-kilo charge of high explosive. The top of the hill erupted and human flesh and blood was blasted, burned and shredded within a fifteen-yard kill radius.

Bolan rolled to his feet and ran as burning pellets apexed at their arc and began to rain down out of the sky.

The flare was floating down low in the sky, hurling long and concealing shadows. Small-arms fire still cracked and popped from the surrounding crown of hills, but the range was extreme for small-caliber rifles firing at night. Bolan made it into the trees. He turned and swept his scope across the valley floor and the hill, but no pursuit was visible. Greenery snapped close by and Bolan brought his rifle on target.

Singh voice spoke in the darkness. "It is I, my friend."

"You all right?"

The big man was little more than a dark shape beneath the trees. "No, I have been shot in the leg and the face, actually."

"Can you walk?"

"I walked here."

"Take a breather. I'll go collect Lily." Bolan looked back at the crown of hills. The gunfire had died off as the enemy took in the damage inflicted by Bolan and Singh. The truth was it was pretty extensive.

Again the *subedar* read Bolan's mind. "If they split into two teams, then we have effectively wiped out two of them. Success or failure, we have much to be proud of."

Singh was right, but Bolan had no time to admire their handiwork or even the endgame. He could only afford to think of the next step. "Now's the time to move if you can take it. I want to be up in those hills and try to punch through their lines before dawn."

22

Chittagong Hills

"You see any white men about?"

The Bangladeshi man peered up at McCarter and shook his head. "No. You are the first white man in a long time to come here."

"Hmm." McCarter pulled out a fat roll of Bangladeshi notes. "What's your name?"

"I am Harun." The man smiled eagerly.

"Harun, you see anyone unusual at all? I mean that doesn't belong up in these hills?"

"Word is Yahya Jott and his cousins get fat job tracking for some strangers that come out of Thailand."

"And who was paying for Yahya's services?"

"Word is some half-caste China." The man scrutinized the cash. "Word is China was paying in dollars."

"Oh, well. I have some of those, too." McCarter pulled out an even thicker roll of American tens, twenties and fifties and began peeling off bills. "About how many men did this China bloke have?"

"Yahya and his two cousins, about six bad men from hither and yon and about another half-dozen Burmese scum."

McCarter nodded. Tom Marchant had put together a regular Southeast Asian foreign legion. He peeled off more bills. "You know which way they went?"

"They head east for the border, and not hiding their tracks, and those Burmese bastards couldn't if they tried. Regular number-one village-raping, drug-smuggling scum."

That would be U Than and his boys, McCarter thought. "Can you point me in the right direction?"

"Easy! You follow path two kilometers south. Go to Hanta village. That where they leave from. After Hanta village?" Harun eyed the SLR slung over McCarter's shoulder. "Maybe you just go toward sound of gunfire."

McCarter smiled to himself. Unlike most sensible citizens, he had been moving toward the sound of gunfire for most of his adult life. "They on foot?"

Harun made a helpless gesture. "Only way to go, except by helicopter, elephant or mule."

McCarter's eye was instantly drawn to a pen beside Harun's house. Within the pen were two water buffaloes calmly chewing their cuds and a raw-boned donkey that looked like a stick figure out of some Neanderthal cave painting giving the two oxen sour looks. McCarter needed to make some time. He had been involved in guerrilla warfare on six continents, and he knew something about donkeys and mules. "That's a handsome jack-mammoth you have there, Harun."

Harun shook his head. "He a piece of shit, but I still need him."

McCarter pulled out his wad of Bangladeshi currency. "These *taka* notes are shit, too, but I have—" he flipped through the dog-eared cash "—about sixty-eight hundred? And I don't need them."

At current exchange rates, sixty-eight hundred *taka* amounted to about a thousand dollars American. Harun snatched the wad from McCarter's hand eagerly. "Piece of shit mule yours. Take him in good health!"

"Thanks, mate. Nice doing business." McCarter shouldered his three packs and walked over to the pen. He regarded the donkey. The buck-toothed, rabbit-eared beast regarded him. It was not love at first sight. Harun called out happily, "His name is Omar."

McCarter peered deeply into Omar's openly hostile brown eyes. "I'll name you Roy."

Roy's lips skinned back from gigantic yellow teeth, but he wasn't smiling.

SIKANDER SINGH WAS almost cross-eyed as he stared out into some middle distance where someone was not stitching his face together without the benefit of anesthetics. Bolan pierced the right side of Singh's chin and noted that the big Indian didn't flinch. "You in your happy place, big man?"

"I assure you I am not," Singh muttered out of the right corner of his mouth.

The bullet had torn a long furrow along his left jaw, scoring the bone and exiting below his earlobe. He was lucky. A millimeter higher and to the left, and it would have taken off his mandible and most of his cheekbone. The wound in his leg had been super-ficial, as well. The Chinese round had been a needle-pointed armor-piercing bullet, and at a range of over fifteen hundred meters had expended most of its energy. It was undoubtedly unpleasant, but the bullet had failed to tumble, and the wound was more as if Singh had been stabbed with a pencil rather than shot with an assault rifle. Nevertheless, both wounds had been bloody, and the Sikh officer had already been on borrowed time when it came to endurance.

Singh read Bolan's mind yet again. "When and if I cannot continue, leave me and I will kill as many as I can to buy you and Miss Na time."

Bolan didn't bother to deny reality. This was going to be the final haul, and it would be the worst. He stuck out his hand instead. "As long as you promise to do the same."

Singh clasped Bolan's hand but held it like a vise rather than shaking. "On one condition."

"Name it."

"The next time? You are going to fire for effect."

Bolan shrugged. "I can't promise that."

"You know, I knew you were going to say that."

Bolan shrugged. "Truth hurts."

"I will have you know being shot in the face also hurts."

Bolan nodded. "I know."

"Yes…" Singh sighed in defeat. "I suppose you do." The big man rose to his feet with a grunt. "So we punch through."

Bolan looked westward. The Chittagong Hills were green lumps in the distance. "Yeah."

"You are worried."

"Yeah."

Singh shrugged. "My friend, we have destroyed two of their three teams. We have gone far further than anyone could have credited us."

"Yeah."

Singh's eyes narrowed sagely. "You are worried about the Chinese sniper."

Bolan gazed across the rolling countryside. The fact was the man had the better rifle with a better scope, and the PRC wouldn't have sent him to retrieve their nuclear defense secrets if he wasn't a crackerjack shot with a number of kills under his belt. The sniper was out there. Bolan could feel him, and he was waiting for Bolan and his battered team to limp into range. "Yeah."

"Very well!" The *subedar* snarled in mock impatience. "If it makes you feel any better? When the time comes, I will fire for effect."

Bolan smiled slyly. "You're a good man, Singh."

"Yes," Singh agreed, shaking his head, "so I am."

CAPTAIN DAI WAS FRUSTRATED. He had lost two of his three teams, and now their one surviving tracker, a Nagar Company private named Hla, insisted that somehow the trio had gotten through their line. Dai had two helicopters, but their fuel reserves were running dangerously low. He had stripped both aircraft of one of their doorgunners to reinforce the hunting teams on the ground, and both machine gunners had been killed for the trouble.

That was the least of Dai's problems. Hla could not meet Dai's eyes as he also insisted that they were now officially encroaching into the sovereign territory of Bangladesh. Dai could not afford to fly his helicopters into Bangladeshi airspace. They would have to catch the American the old-fashioned way and put boots to ground. As far as Dai was concerned, he spit on the ancestors of every Bangladeshi born beneath the vault of heaven, but Beijing had given him his orders. The latest problem was that Captain Phyu was Burmese, and he and his few remaining men were balking at invading their western neighbor.

Hla flinched beneath Captain Dai's glare. "You are certain they have passed through our line?"

Hla slid a glance at Phyu.

"Do not look at him!" Dai snarled. "Look at me when I speak to you!"

"Yes, Captain!" Hla just about jumped out of his combat boots. "I am certain. Sometime in the late afternoon, somehow, they snuck through."

Phyu said nothing as Dai usurped his command. The Nagar Company captain knew he was out of his league and literally out of his territory. He was likely to be in a great deal of trouble with his superiors, and only Captain Dai and his expense account could get him out of it.

Dai fumed. There had to be a silver lining in this situation. "You are a tracker?"

"Yes, Captain."

"What can you tell by the tracks?"

Hla visibly sagged with relief as this went from an interrogation and into his area of expertise. "The big man, the Sikh, he walks with a limp, and I have found blood sign in his footprints. The woman walks unsteadily. I believe she is injured. Judging by their tracks, they cannot be more than an hour ahead of us."

"And the American?"

"He leads, light-footed and sure. Were it not for his comrades, he might well elude us."

Dai nodded. There was the silver lining. There was reason why American Special Forces so widely were feared. They literally measured up to, and sometimes exceeded, the terrible movies Hollywood made about them that were so popular all over the world. But in the end, the Americans were Americans. They were cowboys and lived by their Yankee commando cowboy creed. An intelligent operator, like Dai himself, would have taken the laptop, by force if necessary, and abandoned his companions to disappear into the forest. The American was operating under the admirable but often logistically and sometimes suicidal creed of "No man left behind."

Dai turned to his sniper. "Can you beat this man?"

Private Su thought very long and hard about some of the shots the American appeared to have made. He patted his JS rifle. "He has one of the German semiautomatic weapons he commandeered from the Burmese sharpshooter. My weapon has the longer range by at least two hundred meters, as well as the more powerful optic and is inherently more accurate. Given the shot, I can take him."

Dai eyed his sharpshooter shrewdly. "Yet you are worried."

Su sighed, squared his shoulders and met his commanding officer's eyes. "This American worries me, Captain."

Dai almost smiled. The sharpshooter from Szechwan Province was so earnestly honest it was refreshing. "Su?"

The private steeled himself for the rebuke. "Yes, Captain?"

"This man worries me, too. I will endeavor to provide you with the shot."

Su beamed and snapped off a Beijing parade-ground-worthy salute. "Thank you, Captain!"

Dai snapped a salute back and turned to Captain Phyu. He jerked his head and the two men walked off a little bit. "Did you know my father hunted tigers?"

"No." Phyu was clearly impressed.

"Yes. In the last century, there was still a sizeable number in the Hengduan Shan mountains." Dai shrugged. "They are rumored to be extinct there now."

"A bold occupation. It is clear that valor runs in your family," Phyu said diplomatically.

Dai accepted the compliment. "He hunted them with the tiger fork. One only sees it now in demonstrations of southern-style kung fu. It is like a trident."

Phyu raised a noncommittal eyebrow. "Ah?"

"He always had a saying."

"Oh?"

"Yes, when you hunt tigers in the mountains, you will lose hounds."

Phyu saw where this was going. "We have lost many, many hounds already."

"Yes, but the Sikh is wounded. The woman is injured, and my sniper needs the shot."

"You suggest we ignore all risk and run them down, accept any losses when they must finally turn and fight, and your man will wait for the American to expose himself."

"That is exactly what I am proposing."

Captain Phyu's face openly said what he thought of the plan.

Dai was tempted to slap it, but he did it verbally instead. "My government does not pay a single *yuan* for failure."

Captain Ohnmar Phyu knew who was filling his rice bowl with silver. "Very well. We have clear tracks and blood sign. I will have Hla and my men track them at the run. We will undoubtedly run into an ambush. Have your sniper somewhat behind and ready. When the battle comes, it will come fast and furious."

These were all things Dai knew, but he wanted to hear Phyu say them.

"Also," Phyu continued, "is the woman's life important?"

"My government very much wants to speak with her."

"As long as we acquire that which she carries, if she is shot through the vitals and dies screaming, is this acceptable?"

Dai instantly made his decision. "Indeed, in such a situation I believe the American would sacrifice himself to defend her."

"And the American? The Sikh?"

"Were they taken alive, as with the woman, my government would be grateful. Nevertheless, if nothing but the information the woman has is recovered or destroyed, the gratitude of my nation to those who were of assistance would be boundless."

Captain Phyu nodded as he came to his own decision. "Then let us run down these dogs at once. I shall lead with Hla from the point."

"Excellent."

One of Phyu's men named Chit came running up breathlessly from his position on point. "Captain!"

Phyu scowled. "What is it?"

"I have found a trail!"

"What do you mean? Has the American diverged from the path?"

"No, I believe it a game trail."

"What about it?" Phyu snapped impatiently.

Chit pointed up into the hills. "It goes a hundred meter toward the top of the hills, and then parallels." Chit was very excited. "Do you see?"

The trail could not be seen through the impenetrable greenery, but Chit's finger made a snaking line along the hills. Phyu could indeed see. The trail would not only allow them to get ahead of the American but above him.

Dai saw it, as well. "Su, take the trail! Go as swiftly as possible! Contact me as soon as you spy the American, but I authorize you to take any and all shots of opportunity!"

"Yes, Captain. Thank you." Private Su raised his hand. "Captain?"

"Yes, Private."

Su looked down at his boots. "My observer is dead."

Dai nodded. A sniper team consisted of the shooter and observer or spotter. Su was going after a master marksman with only half a sniper team. Dai hefted his QBZ assault rifle with its 3X optic. "I am not such a bad shot, and I would be honored to serve as your spotter."

Private Su looked as if he might burst into flames.

Dai looked at his opposite number. "Give us a fifteen-minute head start."

Phyu nodded. "Very well. Chit, you will come with me on point with Hla."

Dai turned to Su. "Come, let us go hunt tigers."

23

The enemy was minutes behind them. Bolan had seen them at
the top of the last hill they had climbed and he was fairly sure the
enemy had seen them, as well. They were well within the borders
of Bangladesh, and the Chinese coalition showed no signs of
stopping. There would be no safe haven in Bangladesh until they
were within the walls of the U.S. Embassy. Bolan examined his
team. Singh was limping. Lily was stumbling. Bolan took out
Singh's satellite radio and made the call. "Base, this is Striker,
over."

"Striker! Sitrep," Kurtzman demanded.

"I'm in the Chittagong Hills. My team is in bad shape. I have
hostiles in close pursuit to the east. We can't outrun them. We
make our stand here."

"Striker, be advised. You have hostiles moving toward you from
the west. We believe they are being led by the mole. The Pentagon
has heard rumors of a major player in Asia who is involved in the
heroin trade and selling secrets. The only thing we knew about him
was the code name Variance. We have every reason to believe this
is him, and he's one of ours. He's CIA and started off in local
control and wet work. Consider him extremely dangerous."

Things just kept getting better and better. "Composition of
hostiles?"

"We are guessing squad strength. Maybe half a dozen paramilitary operators or mercs. We have confirmation that U Than
and another half-dozen of his enforcers are with them."

"Any good news?"

"Phoenix leader is on the ground and heading toward you.

He's behind the mole. I have your position triangulated. I'll vector him in."

"Phoenix leader?" It was good news, but Bolan had really wanted to hear that it was Phoenix Force instead.

"He volunteered himself. Our Bangladesh assets are even thinner than Burma."

It would have to be enough, and David McCarter was force multiplier unto himself. The hard part would be staying alive until got there. "Copy that, Base. Keep me advised. Striker out."

SINGH STOOD BENT OVER with hands on knees. Blood stained his leg from his hip to his ankle. The rocket launcher lay across his shoulders like a yoke.

"You want to lighten that load?" Bolan asked.

Singh raised a weary eyebrow. "You have no idea."

Lily sagged to her knees with a groan. The pistol in her hand looked as if it weighed a mountain. Bolan gave her some water and got her back on her feet. "I want you to go down the path a little ways, go around the bend and get into the trees."

Lily wordlessly stumbled off in the direction Bolan had pointed. He turned to the matter at hand. "You hit them as the main body comes around the far bend in the trail. Depending which way they split, I'll hit the survivors with the grenade launcher."

"It is as sound a plan as any." Singh sighed heavily as he dropped to a knee and aimed the rocket launcher through the shrubbery. Bolan slung his sniper rifle and hefted the automatic weapon with the grenade launcher beneath it. The two warriors waited in silence. Long minutes passed. Singh knelt as still as a stone as he kept his eye fixed through the rocket launcher's optic. "We should have seen them by now."

Bolan checked his watch. The enemy was late. Something was going on.

"I detect motion," the big man said. He brought his eye closer to his optic. "Yes, they come."

Bolan watched as the tracker came into view followed by two men with rifles. They were moving swiftly, almost as if they were unafraid of ambush. Bolan and Singh waited until they came into range and continued waiting. Six more men appeared leaving a good hundred yards between themselves and the point team. One of the six bore a light machine gun and another a rocket launcher like Singh's. Bolan's eyes narrowed. He didn't like the point team getting this close, but his team could no longer run. If the enemy could get either support weapon into range the fight was over.

As expected, the sniper was nowhere in sight. "Whenever you get the notion."

Singh nodded behind his sight, and his finger curled around the trigger and squeezed. The rocket-propelled grenade hissed from the tube in a streak of smoke and fire. "Rocket away!"

Bolan took aim through the ladder sight of the grenade launcher as he watched the rocket streak toward the men on the steep trail. Two of the six men leaped from the trail, braving the almost vertical terrain. The rocket erupted among the remaining four, and fire and smoke occluded them. Bolan's rifle thudded backward against him as the 40 mm launcher fired. The grenade looped through the air and detonated between the two plunging men. Their weapons dropped from their hands and their limbs went boneless as the shrapnel shredded them at point-blank range. The dead men tumbled like bundles of rags down the hill.

The point team had scattered onto the sides of the trail. Singh dropped the smoking tube and reached for the spare rifle. "Drop a grenade where they went to ground and I will—" Singh staggered as if he'd been shoved from behind as a high-powered rifle cracked from above.

"Sikander!" Bolan shouted.

Singh turned and blinked dazedly back up the hillside. A red stain was spreading across his chest. The rifle above cracked a second time. Singh's eyes rolled in his head, and his knees buckled as a second bullet took him through the torso.

"Sikander!" Bolan sprayed a burst up the hill and then dropped low. He grabbed the big man by his shoulder strap and hauled him behind cover.

Singh groaned. "I am…all right."

The *subedar* was far from all right. He was finished. The sniper's bullets had torn through him front to back. One had taken him high in the chest and shattered his collarbone inches from his heart. The lower one had punched low through his side, splintering his ribs and driven the shards through his vitals like shrapnel. Bolan pressed a field dressing against the wounds, but the blood welled up underneath them like an overflowing sink. The ugly fact was that without a real medical officer with a kit containing blood expanders, Singh was going to bleed out in minutes. He wasn't going to walk out of there, and Bolan couldn't carry him.

Despite going into shock Singh was remarkably lucid. "Enough. You must go now, and go quickly. There is nothing you can do for me."

Bolan took out their last ampoule of morphine. Singh waved it away with a palsied hand, but Bolan administered it into his right thigh anyway. Singh made a contented grunt as the narcotic entered his blood. "Well, now, that is a comfort!"

Bolan let out a long breath. "Sikander?"

"Yes, my friend?"

"I gotta go." He drew the Chinese silenced pistol and gazed down at the *subedar*. Singh looked back without flinching. They both knew what Bolan was offering.

Singh smiled and there was blood on his teeth. "I thank you for the thought, but my religion frowns upon suicide and euthanasia. Suffering is part of God's plan. Indeed, no matter how bad the situation, it is one's duty to make the best of it, and that is what I shall do. Leave me my Browning and the two hand grenades on my belt. I will rest a moment or two, and then perhaps I will crawl into the bushes and see what I can arrange for our guests."

Bolan put the pistol away. He drew Singh's pistol for him and cocked it before putting it in his hand. "You take care of yourself, Sikander."

"Indeed, I shall. Now go with God, and go swiftly. Miss Na needs you now more than I."

Bolan turned and loped down the path.

"EXCELLENT!" CAPTAIN DAI clapped Private Su on the shoulder. The sniper specialist beamed with pride. Dai had seen the Sikh take two hits to the torso before collapsing. Su was indeed a master rifleman. There had been no clear shot on the American, but Dai expected one to present itself shortly. The American could not carry the big Indian. If he stood by his wounded companion, he would die. His last rocket was expended, and at any moment he would be carrying the woman. Phyu and his team would hound him, and Dai and Su would wait for the shot.

Dai clicked on his radio. "Captain Phyu, we have one hostile down, the Indian. Do you have a fix on the rocket launch point?"

"Yes," Phyu radioed back. "We saw it quite clearly."

"Proceed to the enemy attack point, confirm the kill."

Phyu was clearly eager for the kill, and eager to get the hell out of Bangladesh. "And if the American is there?"

"The American may be lurking in the vicinity. Approach with caution. If he fires upon you, do not try to overwhelm him. Engage him from a distance, make him fire. Private Su will look for the kill shot. If you can pin him down I will begin a flanking movement from above."

"If he has moved on?"

Dai smiled. That would be even better. He would rather take the American while he was running than try to dig him out of cover while he made his last stand. "If he is moving, he will have the woman on his hands. She will slow him. I will sprint ahead along the trail two kilometers and then descend to get in front of him. Once we have him pinned between us, Private Su will look for the shot."

"I understand. We will begin our approach immediately."

Down below Phyu looked to his men. "Hla! Take point! Chit, stay a little bit back with the grenade launcher."

Captain Phyu's team took their time, moving along the sides of the trail rather than on it. It was a matter of minutes before Hla held up his fist for the team to halt. Phyu crept forward and grinned from ear to ear.

The Indian lay by the side of the trail and he was in a very bad way.

His spent rocket launcher lay a meter away in the mud. His rifle was gone, clearly confiscated by the American. The man lay prone in the mud. Phyu could see the ragged red craters in his back where the big rifle had holed him. The man did not have long to live. One leg pushed feebly. One arm hung limp. He held a pistol in one hand, but he had to submerge it in the mud to drag himself along.

Phyu motioned Hla forward. The Indian noticed the tracker. Twice the big man feebly tried to do a push-up, but he lacked the strength to turn himself over. His pistol pushed through the mud as he tried to lift it, but Hla stepped on his wrist and took it from him.

The tracker took a quick glance around the area. "The American and the woman have moved on. They are heading northwest, but they are not far."

Captain Phyu clicked on his radio. "Dai, we have the Indian. He is alive but mortally wounded. The American and the woman have abandoned him. Hla says they are heading straight down the trail."

"Acknowledged. Kill the man and continue tracking."

Captain Ohnmar Phyu smiled unpleasantly. He had a better idea. His bayonet rasped from its sheath. He had personally captured the Indian special forces officer. His subsequent escape from interrogation was a personal insult that Phyu intended to personally avenge. However, there was strategy to his sadism. Americans were notoriously sentimental people. Captain Phyu had a hunch that big man's agonized screams might just draw the American out. "Dai, have your sniper ready. I believe I can make the American expose himself. He will be moving back toward this position."

Dai saw the plan and apparently he liked it. "Acknowledged."

Phyu nodded to his men. "Hla, keep watch to the north. Chit, come here and assist me." Phyu knelt beside Singh and gave him a long look at the knife. "You are going to sing for me, like a bird."

Singh lifted his head out the mud enough to spit. "I did not sing for you in your camp, nor shall I do so now."

Phyu shook his head happily. They would see how tough the big man was with his manhood removed. "Chit, turn him over and open his pants."

Chit grabbed the big man and heaved him over onto his back. Chit froze in horror as the cotter pins of first the fragmentation grenade and then the white phosphorus pinged away into the bushes. Singh's huge hand shot out and clasped Captain Phyu's ankle in a death grip. His bloody teeth flashed in a smile of savage exultation. Chit lurched to his feet with a wordless shout. Hla turned to see what was going on. Phyu wasted another second of the three-second fuses trying to yank his foot free. Singh waggled his eyebrows up at Phyu insultingly.

"Gotcha!"

The frag grenade detonated and Subedar Sikander Singh slaughtered his enemies and went to meet his Maker. The white phosphorus exploded, and he cremated himself in a somewhat unorthodox fashion. There would be no one to scatter his ashes in the nearest river as was custom, but God and the afternoon rain shower would take care of that. The bend in the path filled with smoke and fire.

Honor and duty had been observed.

CAPTAIN DAI SNARLED into his radio. "Phyu! Come in! Phyu!"

Captain Phyu was not answering the radio. Dai knew quite well the sound of a grenade detonating and he recognized a white-phosphorus cloud when he saw one. Phyu, Hla and Chit were dead. Dai and Private Su were the last men alive. Captain Dai spit. It didn't matter. The math was still the same. The contest was now between a Chinese special forces captain and a sniper specialist versus an exhausted American and an injured whore.

Dai watched as the afternoon breeze carried the billowing hot smoke slowly up the hillside toward them like a huge ghost creeping through the trees. Private Su looked up from his rifle. "I cannot see anything. The American will use the smoke as a screen to run for the next hill. Captain, I suggest now might be the time to run them down."

"Yes, I will take point. His tracks should not be difficult to follow. Hla said he was heading— No!" Dai bolted upright as his instincts kicked in. "He is attacking! He is attacking now!"

As if in answer, orange fire stuttered out of the smoke cloud. Private Su snapped up his rifle for the shot. Dai snarled a second too late. "No!"

Su's JS rifle cracked. A second later yellow fire flared in the phosphorus fog as a grenade launcher thumped in response. Dai sprayed a burst from his rifle and hurled himself behind a tree. Su stood his ground and took another shot at the flash of fire in the smoke. He threw himself aside a moment too late as the grenade landed beside him with unerring accuracy. Su screamed as he was rent and torn by the bee swarm of metal ball bearings. He fell twisting and went on screaming as he writhed in the dirt. "Captain!" Su screamed blindly as he clutched at the pulped sockets of his eyes. His guts were spilled all over him.

Dai let Su go on screaming as he crouched behind the tree. The American would be coming to confirm his kill. The white-phosphorus cloud slowly oozed up the hillside borne on the updraft of the hills, and the first hint of its brimstone stench stung his nostrils. The smoke wasn't thick, but things were shadowy enough beneath the jungle canopy without the shreds of hot smoke twisting through the trees.

"Captain!" Su howled like the damned in hell. "Capt—"

Su went limp in midscream. Dai snapped his rifle around. The captain instantly discerned the fresh bullet hole in the sniper's temple. Dai swung his optic around the horizon frantically. He hadn't heard the shot or seen the muzzle-flash. He refused to believe the American could tote a sniper rifle, an assault rifle with a grenade launcher and his silenced rifle all at the same time, he would— Dai's blood went cold. His gaze snapped back to his sniper. Su had been shot in the temple and there was no exit wound. Private Su hadn't been shot with a rifle; he'd been shot with a silenced pistol. Dai knew exactly what kind. His military manufactured them. They were neither powerful nor particularly accurate, which meant the American was close. Close enough to take Su with a headshot. Close enough to toss a grenade onto Dai's position. Close enough to—

A voice spoke quietly behind him. "You speak English?"

Dai twisted on a double-edged dagger of fear and rage.

The voice was disturbingly conversational. "You're useless to me if you don't."

"I speak English," Dai spit.

"Good. Drop the rifle. Then lose the rest of your weapons. One at a time. Use your left hand, and use two fingers."

Dai divested himself of his armament.

"Stand up. Turn around."

Captain Dai stood and faced the American. He was a captain of a Chinese infiltration unit but even he was intimidated. The man was tall. His face was a mask of smoke, bruising blood and dirt. Worst of all were the man's eyes. His ice-blue gaze burned down unblinkingly at Dai. The captain stood before the white devil.

"You and I need to come to an understanding."

It was hard to gain any moral ground on a man more than a head taller than himself, but Dai squared his shoulders defiantly. "There is nothing to understand. My duty is clear."

"The mole, he's CIA. He's heading this way with half a dozen mercs backed up by U Than and another half dozen of his thugs. He double-dealed against you with Indian intelligence and played both sides against the middle. He intends to sell the data back to your government, as well as to India, Taiwan and the United States. Your duty is clear, and he can't leave you alive to try to stop him."

"I see little difference. You will do the same."

"No, I made a promise. I'm going to give the data to my government, as well as Indian and Taiwanese intelligence."

"Other than being a fool and making no profit, I do not see the difference."

"The difference is we have a fight coming up. You play me square, I'll let you live."

Dai's fists clenched, but he had no immediate retort. He found that life was sweet, and he wanted to continue living it.

"Just so we both know, I've already hidden the laptop. I've radioed my people its location. Even if you kill me, my people will come back later and recover it at their leisure."

Dai made his decision. "Very well. I will fight beside you. I will not try to kill you. You have my word as an officer."

The blue eyes burned into Dai for several moments. "Give me your radio and gear up. We've got to get moving."

Dai handed over his satellite radio and began rearming himself as the American turned his back and examined Private Su's JS rifle speculatively. Captain Dai was an officer and a man of his word. He would assist the American. The mole would die for betraying the People's Republic of China. Nor would Dai try to kill the American. When the time came he would break his bones, tear his tendons and rip the whereabouts of the laptop from his screaming, crippled flesh.

After that he would let the jungle kill him.

24

"What have you got, Tito?" Marchant scanned the hills from a hilltop vantage as Tuilosega and two of his men examined the battle scene.

Tuilosega radioed back. "Back along the trail you got four burned and blasted bodies. Looks like a rocket hit. You got two more bodies below at the bottom of the gully. Looks like they got taken by shrapnel. Hard to tell but they all look to be Burmese or Chinese. Looks like they got bushwhacked but good."

"What about the smoke site?"

"Well, as you can probably tell, that was white phosphorus. We got four bodies on the trail. They're just about burned beyond recognition, 'cept that three are small and one is gigantic. Like about my size. I'm betting that's the Sikh."

"What else?"

"Yahya followed a track up the hillside and found a dead Chinese. The interesting thing is that he found two tracks leading away from him. One is definitely the American."

Marchant frowned. "Is the second track the woman?"

"No. Combat boots. Yahya has his cousin Mahmood following them now. The woman's tracks lead farther down the path to the west. Cousin Saquib is following that one."

"Which way does Yahya think they are trying to go?"

"He thinks they've probably already linked up. As to which way they're going? The only way to go is west, but he doesn't think they got past us."

"He's right." Marchant stared out at the sea of rolling green hills. They suddenly looked a lot more menacing. "They didn't go anywhere. They're right here. Right here among us. Tell Mahmood and Saquib to report in every five minutes."

SAQUIB BARELY HAD TIME to blink before the tomahawk hit him. Bolan had thrown sidearm, and the titanium scythed through his lips, teeth and tongue and crunched to a stop against the cartilage in the back of his throat. The U Than man beside him started in horror only to have Captain Dai emerge from the foliage beside him. Dai's snake hands pistoned in three quick finger strikes, first to one side of the gangster's throat with the second and third blows directly into the hollow of his throat. The drug muscle's machine gun fell from his hands as dropped to the ground and went into strangling convulsions. The third man raised his weapon but not before Bolan expended one of his three remaining silenced rounds into his forehead.

Dai examined the bodies. "Bangladeshi, Burmese…" He squinted over the merc. "By his tattoos I would say this man is Thai."

Bolan retrieved his tomahawk. "We have to move. The tracking team looking for Lily will be on her any minute."

"Yes…the woman." Dai clearly thought the woman expendable.

Bolan was beginning to suspect Dai would observe the letter of their understanding but felt no loyalty to its spirit. He kept his suspicions to himself as he unslung his scout rifle and they doubled back down along high path. They had moved Lily farther down the path and then had been forced to carry her halfway up the hill. Bolan loped to his chosen sniper hide with Dai on his heels. Another three-man tracking team was working its way up. Bolan dropped into a rifleman's squat, winding his sling around his arm and propping his elbow on his knee to form a solid shooting platform. The range was around 150 meters. Bolan put his crosshairs on the tracker and squeezed the trigger. The little scout made no more noise than a hiccup.

The tracker let out a high-pitched scream and tumbled backward clutching his neck as blood sprayed between his fingers. The gangster behind him screamed as the man fell into him and arterial spray painted his face. Bolan ignored the thug and swept his sight onto the merc. He had been going for the head shot on the tracker. The past few days had been very hard on the scout rifle, and his optics seemed to be slightly off. The merc was wearing soft body armor that would defeat the slow-moving subsonic ammo. Bolan took an extra heartbeat to raise his sights to the crown of the merc's skull and fired.

The merc's forehead crumpled like an eggshell and he flopped like a boned fish to the forest floor.

U Than's boy had disentangled himself from the bleeding out tracker and he was still screaming as he blindly sprayed the landscape. Bolan let him scream and shoot. The noise would help cover his movement. He moved down the hillside to Lily's hide. A tree had uprooted and left a pocket in the hillside hidden by its shattered trunk. Lily sat curled in a fetal ball shaking and weeping. Her turban was unspooling down her head, and the fish-white skin of her stubbled skull peeked through in places. Her face was ghostly pale where it wasn't covered with dirt. She clutched at her broken arm, for which there was no morphine.

Even now she was heartbreakingly beautiful.

Bolan spoke quietly. "Hey, hot sarong. How's it going?"

Lily pushed at the tears streaking her face with the heel of her hand. The Hi-Power pistol she held pushed up against her turban and a loop of fabric fell down across her eyes. Her voice shook as she shoved the material aside. "Not very well, actually."

"It's almost over. We've whittled down Variance and his team by five already. Dai and I are going to play a few more games with them and then go for the big kill, and the cavalry is coming."

"The cavalry?"

"Well, more of an Englishman, but you'll like him."

Lily laughed despite herself.

Lily sighed. "Maybe I'll like him, but I hate Burma."

"Actually you're in Bangladesh."

"I hate Bangladesh," she responded. "I hate my job." She stared up at Bolan and shook her head. "I hate you."

Bolan shrugged. "I know."

Lily half laughed and half sobbed on the ragged edge of hysteria.

"Tell the bitch to be quiet," Dai snarled.

Bolan turned to look up at the captain. Dai flinched beneath Bolan's eyes.

Lily spoke first. "The captain is correct. I will be quiet."

Bolan jerked his head at Dai. "Let's move."

TUILOSEGA SOUNDED CLOSE to panic. "I can't raise either tracking team! We just lost six and it was done silent! There's some spooky-ass shit going on!"

Marchant watched from his hilltop redoubt as one of U Than's men crashed through the underbrush covered with blood and screaming at the top of his lungs. He was heading south and didn't look as if he was going to stop until he reached the Bay of Bengal. "We lost five."

U Than busily punched numbers in his cell phone.

Tuilosega still wasn't happy. "This American asshole is a fucking ghost! And he's ghosting us!"

"Someone's helping him, and if I had to bet, it's that goddamn Dai." Marchant clicked over his receiver to the captain's private frequency. "Dai, what do you think you're doing?"

Marchant was rewarded as the captain's voice spoke over the radio. "Positioning myself to send your soul to hell."

"Is the American nearby?"

Dai paused long seconds. "No, he has Private Su's sniper rifle. He is taking the high ground to get the shot on a cluster of your mercenaries. I am staying closer to hit them with grenades."

Marchant smelled a rat. "That's awfully informative of you, Dai."

"You seek to sell the data back to my government, as well as that of the United States, India and Taiwan."

Marchant didn't deny it. "And?"

"And I can give you the American right now," Dai replied.

Things weren't quite going according to plan, and Marchant had to admit it was an intriguing offer. "And in return I could expect…?"

"One, you would live."

"I need a little more than that, Dai."

"Two, my government will still be grateful. May I suggest to you that once one's fortunes run over a billion dollars, how many billion starts to become somewhat irrelevant. The money from my government is assured, and so is your survival if you agree."

"Not a bad deal. Tell me where the American is." Again Marchant smelled a rat. He put his palm over the receiver and turned to Jimmy Sukarno. "Jimmy, find out where the hell Tito is and have him and his men fall back to the hill. I want to be able to put a shitstorm on the American's position once we have him designated."

The Indonesian rose from his hide and scanned the hills below them. He pointed below. "Tito's about two hundred meters below us." Jimmy picked up his own radio. "Tito, we need you to—"

Jimmy Sukarno's head exploded like a melon.

Marchant threw himself flat and instantly knew what had happened. Dai had gone chatty to keep him on the radio. The American had his own people scanning the frequency, and they had triangulated on his position. Marchant thumbed his frequency over. "Tito, fall back. Head west. We need a skirmishing line set up in the cleft between the hills."

Below a grenade launcher thumped. A second later he heard screams as men were torn. Tuilosega gasped over the radio. "I'm hit. Yahya and Arturo are gone!"

"How many of U Than's men do you have left?"

"They're fucking running for the trees. They're…oh, shit—"

A rifle shot slammed over the radio and the connection went dead.

Marchant turned and roared at U Than. The Burmese drug lord was hugging dirt with his men. "We fall back." He pointed back the way they had come. "The cleft in the hills. Leave some of your men to defend it. You and I will move back and I'll organize more mercenaries. I can have them here in an hour."

U Than rose brandishing a pistol in his hand, but he got the plan. He shouted at his men, who also got the plan and didn't seem to appreciate it.

A rifle cracked behind them from the bottom of the hill, and U Than stumbled, went slack-jawed and fell with a ragged hole through his chest. The rifle cracked three more times in rapid-fire, and U Than's three remaining goons dropped like cattle at the top of the slaughter chute. Marchant sprayed his H&K subgun into the trees at the bottom of the hill but he hadn't seen the shooter. How the hell the American had gotten behind him so quickly was—

A voice boomed from the top of the hill, "Drop it!"

Marchant's jaw worked but no sound came out. The American hadn't been behind him, but he was behind him now. A Caucasian man came out of the trees at the bottom of the hill. He carried an SLR rifle with an optic sight, and Marchant stared down its barrel. The man spoke with an English accent. "The man said drop it! You don't, and I'll bloody well cut you in two!"

Marchant dropped his subgun. He turned backward and Captain Dai and the scariest white dude he had ever seen in his life stood at the crest of the hill. The big guy held a Chinese sniper rifle at his shoulder, and the muzzle was pointed at Marchant's middle. "Lose the pistol."

Marchant drew his Smith & Wesson and dropped it to the dirt.

Lily Na tottered over the top of the hill. One arm was in a sling. A turban hung in an unraveling mess over her razor-stubbled head. In one hand she held a pistol and her green eyes glared at Marchant. Lily, Dai and the American walked down the hill with weapons ready as the Englishman marched up. Marchant was unarmed and between the hammer and the anvil. His mind blurred as he tried to come up with a survival strategy.

He turned to the American. "Listen, I know things you want to know. About China, Southeast Asia, heroin routes and connections, moles in U.S. intelligence and—"

"And that's why you're breathing," Bolan agreed. "You're coming back to the States. You're going to spill. You do that, and

I'll exert every bit of influence I have to see that you don't get the death penalty."

Marchant swallowed with difficulty. "Listen, I—"

Captain Dai's rifle ripped into full automatic fire. He held down his trigger and the traitor twisted, jerked and fell as Dai burned a 30-round magazine into him. Dai's rifle clacked open on empty. Bolan and McCarter swung their weapons on him, but Dai lowered the muzzle and calmly reloaded.

Bolan stared at Dai coldly. "You know, I really wanted to talk with him."

"You know, I really do not want my country's ballistic missile technology to fall into the hands of the United States, India and Taiwan, but that is the way things are," Dai countered. "Variance betrayed me and my government, as well. You will forgive me if I take a measure of payback."

Bolan's, McCarter's and Lily's weapons didn't waver.

Dai sighed and shook his head. "Very well." The captain dropped his rifle to the ground. He drew his pistol with two fingers of his left hand and dropped it to join his assault weapon. "I am at your mercy, but with your permission I will follow you to Dhaka and the Chinese consulate there."

McCarter raised an eyebrow at Bolan. It was a long trek out of the Chittagong Hills and a lot could happen along the trail. It was pretty clear the Englishman thought Dai needed killing.

Bolan had given his word. "Fair enough, Captain. You did your bit. Gear up."

Dai bent to pick up his rifle. Bolan saw stars as Dai's foot rocketed up beneath his chin and his rifle fell from his hands. Dai spun and the knife edge of his hand chopped into the side of McCarter's neck. The Englishman's eyes rolled and he dropped as if he'd been shot. Dai spun again and the back of his hand cracked across Lily's face and sprawled her to the ground. Bolan saw the Chinese captain through a long tunnel with purple sparks around the edges as he tried to draw the silenced Chinese assassination pistol. A foot he never saw kicked it out his hands. Dai spun and his boot blasted the air out of Bolan's lungs. The big American fell backward but as he did he rolled.

Bolan rolled, spitting blood and reaching for his knife and tomahawk.

Dai was already bending to retrieve his rifle. The tomahawk flashed from Bolan's fist and revolved through the air at Dai's head. Dai sinuously snapped his head and shoulders aside and the ax flashed past. Bolan threw his knife as he closed. It was a weak throw but no one stood by and let a flying knife hit them. Dai twisted aside as he rose out of his crouch. Bolan threw all of his weight into a flying tackle that Dai couldn't dodge.

The two men met with bone-breaking force. Bolan's size and weight told, and they hit the ground in a whirl of limbs. Dai might have been a snake-hand kung fu exponent but now they were down in the dirt, and Bolan knew something about ground fighting. He slammed his elbow down into Dai face and twisted his hips to block the knee Dai rammed up between his legs. Dai's stiffened finger ripped through Bolan's eyebrow like a cold chisel a centimeter from his eyeball.

Dai twisted and writhed beneath Bolan, and the Executioner grimaced as a second knee strike toward his groin gave him the horrid ache of a near miss. Bolan tried for another elbow, but Dai's limbs were everywhere, smothering his every effort. Bolan was larger, stronger and had the mount but Dai was winning. Bolan was managing to save his eyes but Dai's finger strikes were everywhere. Beneath Bolan's ear, under his jaw and in the side of his neck paralyzing pain blossomed and flared. Dai got a thumb into Bolan's left inner elbow, and the Executioner's arm went numb to the wrist. Dai's hand got close to Bolan's ear and his little finger suddenly bored inward, violating Bolan's aural canal and twisting to rupture the eardrum. Bolan yanked his head away, and Dai's other hand split into a peace symbol and shot for his eyes. Dai barely missed but fresh blood exploded out of the cut over Bolan's left eye.

Bolan slammed his two hundred pounds back down, leading with his forehead.

Dai's nose and cheekbone fractured beneath the blow. Bolan rose and drove his head down a second and a third time. Colors swam across Bolan's vision as he turned Dai's head sideways with his functioning hand and pinned it to the dirt. He lifted his head and then slammed it down a final time. The thin bone of Dai's temple fractured and caved beneath the blow.

Bolan sat back and watched the world spin as Dai shuddered and twitched. McCarter pushed himself up and stared at Bolan sheepishly as he held his face. The left side of his head from his ear to his jaw was turning black and swelling like a balloon. He held his Hi-Power in a shaky hand. He lowered it as Dai bled from his ears and tear ducts beneath Bolan.

"Sorry about that, Mack. I swear the little bugger could give Bruce Lee a run for his money."

"Yeah." Bolan pushed himself up with a groan, and fresh waves of a psychedelic light show swam across his vision. He put hand on a tree trunk to steady himself. "I know." Bolan walked over to Lily and helped her up. Her face was in about the same shape as Bolan's and McCarter's.

Bolan smiled out of a mask of blood. "You look hot."

The functioning corner of Lily's mouth twitched upward. "You are a sick man."

"Yeah, I get that a lot." Bolan watched as McCarter led his ride out from the trees. "That's one ugly ass mule you got there."

"He's a donkey," McCarter corrected. "His name is Roy. I'm keeping him."

Lily stared at the filthy beast in wonder. "You said the cavalry was coming. I didn't believe you."

"I get that a lot, too," Bolan admitted. He winced at the ache as he tilted his head toward Roy. It was two hundred miles to Dhaka. "Your chariot awaits. Let's get you home."

TAKE 'EM FREE

2 action-packed novels plus a mystery bonus

NO RISK

NO OBLIGATION TO BUY

James Axler
Outlanders®

SERPENT'S TOOTH

A combination of reptilian and human DNA, the Najah are the revitalized foot soldiers of the Earth's ancient alien masters, the Annunaki. Surviving the megacull of humanity, these half-cobra warriors vow to avenge their near extinction and usher in a new age on Earth. From its underground war base in northern India, this monstrous force launches its cleansing fire. Kane and his allies have one hope—a renegade female Najah, reptilian and ruthless, whose alliance is both a promise…and a threat.

Available February wherever books are sold.

POLAR QUEST
by AleX Archer

When archaeologist Annja Creed agrees to help an old colleague on a dig in Antarctica, she wonders what he's gotten her into. Her former associate has found a necklace made of an unknown metal. He claims it's over 40,000 years old—and that it might not have earthly origins. As the pair conduct their research, Annja soon realizes she has more to worry about than being caught in snowslides. With no one to trust and someone out to kill her, Annja has nowhere to turn—and everything to lose.

Available January wherever books are sold.